GHOSTHUNTERS

Haunted School

Anthony Masters

ORCHARD BOOKS

To the staff and pupils of Eastbrook
Comprehensive School, Dagenham, Essex,
with affectionate memories of their outstanding
creative work

Acc. no. T08373

Class. F/MAS

ORCHARD BOOKS
96 Leonard Street, London EC2A 4RH
Orchard Books Australia
14 Mars Road, Lane Cove, NSW 2066
First published in Great Britain in 1996
First paperback publication 1996
© Anthony Masters 1996
The right of Anthony Masters to be identified as the
Author of this Work has been asserted by him in accordance
with the Copyright, Designs and Patents Act, 1988.
A CIP catalogue record for this book is available
from the British Library
1 85213 895 5 (hardback)
1 86039 070 6 (paperback)
Printed in Great Britain

CHAPTER ONE

"You can see through that dog," said Jenny, her voice wobbling and her eyes fixed rigidly in front of her as if she were trying to bring something into focus.

"What?" David turned towards his sister. She had dragged him away from his football game and he was cross, out of breath and wanted to go back. "What dog?"

"Over there."

David went cold all over as the shock hit him. He suddenly felt sick. Sweat broke out on his forehead and his hands felt clammy. She was right; he could see through the Labrador – straight through to the banners behind. They read *SAVE HOCKLEY ANIMAL SANCTUARY. NOW.* But he was riveted by the see-through dog. It couldn't be happening. The dog couldn't be happening. Not like that. There must be some explanation, but what?

"I don't believe it!" he said, trembling.

"Neither do I," agreed Jenny. "It must be a trick of the light."

The Labrador was wandering about in the playground, occasionally leaping up at a passing ball and the light was quite normal for England – sunny but with a hint of rain. There weren't any tricks.

"What do the others think?" David stared around him, hoping for support.

"They can't see him," his twin replied. "They'd all be talking about it if they could."

"They must be able to," David protested, although he knew she was right. But why couldn't anyone see the Labrador except them? And what was more, the playground and its occupants seemed to be shifting, becoming insubstantial, there but not quite there. What was going on? It was as if they weren't in the right time – or any time.

"Why don't you ask Gary?" Jenny said urgently and he could feel her fear. "Why don't you ask him if he's noticed the dog?"

"No way." The feeling of being disconnected was getting worse, much worse, and he could see Jenny was feeling exactly the same.

Their eyes returned to the Labrador who was jumping for another ball. Then he loped over to the banners that had been set up in the playground by one of the teachers. The school had been running a series of events in aid of the Animal Sanctuary which had been running out of funds for a long time and had finally reached crisis point.

If they didn't receive a large influx of funds by the end of the month they would have to close.

At eleven years old the twins were still very close – close enough to realise without having to put it into words that the normality around them had been horribly interfered with.

"Only we can see that dog," David gasped.

"Looks like it." Jenny gazed back at him, her brown eyes and thatch of dark hair almost identical to his own. "Pull yourself together," she whispered. "Everyone will think you've gone crazy."

"Maybe I have," he muttered. The growing feeling of apartness, of not being in the playground at all, was even more terrifying than the see-through dog. It was rather as if he were watching a film of kids playing – and he was in the audience.

Suddenly, the Labrador was running towards them, his eyes lighting up as if he knew them. He jumped up and began to lick her face. Then he did the same to David. They could both feel the dog's breath, but when they tried to touch him, their hands went straight through his fur – into nothing at all.

"What are you doing?" asked Gary, coming up panting, ball in hand. His round, freckled face topped with straggling ginger hair looked puzzled in the May sunshine. Then the puzzlement turned to mockery. "You two gone bananas?"

With a lurch, David and Jenny saw the children in the playground had jumped back into focus, and they had a sense of re-joining, of belonging again.

"No." David scowled. Gary had a mean streak. Anything that was a little bit different Gary seized on and sneered at – and what David and Jenny had experienced was more than a little bit different. There was no way he was going to expose it to Gary's ferret-like probing.

As casually as he could, David shrugged his shoulders, and to his relief the Labrador jumped down and nuzzled a stick on the hot tarmac.

"So what were you doing waving your arms about?"

"Nothing much," replied David, going red.

"Push off, Gary." Jenny could be very fierce at times, particularly with boys, and most of them were secretly afraid of her. But Gary sensed he had an advantage so he stood his ground, grinning unpleasantly.

"You into doing a bit of dancing then, Dave? Thinking of joining Miss Tivett's Dance Club? Going to do a bit of ballet and tap?"

But David was saved by the bell from having to reply.

"Line up," yelled Mr Spurgeon. "Line up. Now!"

To their consternation, David and Jenny saw the Labrador lining up too.

★

The see-through dog sat down behind Mr Spurgeon and began to lick itself while he talked about next term's school trip to the Thames estuary and the wildlife he hoped they'd be able to see there. He could make even the most interesting subjects boring, and while Mr Spurgeon droned on Jenny felt herself getting sleepy. The feeling of apartness, of being somewhere else had gone, but the shock of it all – and the sheer lack of any rational explanation – had left her exhausted. Jenny had always shared thoughts and intuition with her twin, so she was not surprised that they had shared the same alarming sensation. Although it helped that they had experienced it together, there was something quite terrifying about a see-through dog. She tried to concentrate, to take in what Mr Spurgeon was saying, but it was no good. However hard she fought, Jenny found her eyes kept closing, and when she glanced back at David she could see that his were too.

She was also feeling rather chilly. A new stab of fear made her heart beat furiously, her hands and feet were icy, her eyelids like lead, forcing themselves to close.

In her mind's eye, Jenny saw the bulky figure of her mother's Great Uncle Arthur. She recognised him immediately although he had died years ago –

sometime at the end of the Second World War. There were photographs in the house and he was an unforgettable character in his big shiny suit and trilby hat, with a large black bristling moustache and eyes that laughed out at you in a mocking sort of way. She had always been a little frightened of him because he seemed so much larger than life – as if he were very powerful. At least, that's what the photographs told her.

Arthur was a legend in the Golding household. He had been a crook – a thief in fact, but a thief with a difference, for he frequently gave away some of his loot to the poor. He loved animals and had donated a large sum to the Animal Sanctuary which had opened up some years before the war, but as Jenny and David's mother had said, "He was a villain through and through – don't be fooled by his Robin Hood act."

Arthur was standing on a flight of stone steps and yelling up at her angrily, but she couldn't hear a word he was saying. Then his image faded, her eyes snapped back open and she could see the see-through dog licking Mr Spurgeon's trousers. She felt fear twist in her again. What was happening? What had Arthur been trying to say to her? She glanced quickly back at David. He gave her a frightened look and Jenny knew he had seen exactly what she had just seen. What did all this mean, she wondered. The appearance of the ghost dog – for that's what she was sure the Labrador was – the horrible feeling of isolation, of watching the present from somewhere else. But where? And now this dream – or vision – of Arthur. Why was he so angry?

David was as scared and as bewildered as his sister. He couldn't understand what was going on. He too had felt sleepy and had also seen Arthur standing on the stone steps yelling up at him.

He badly wanted to talk to Jenny. She could calm him down, make him feel safe, and that's what he wanted to feel now.

"David Golding!"

Mr Spurgeon's usually tired, pale blue eyes were fixed piercingly upon him.

"Yes, sir?"

"You were asleep."

"No—"

"I saw you asleep."

Out of the corner of his eye David could see Gary grinning again. He'd really fix him one day.

"No, sir."

"Are you calling me a liar?"

"No, sir. I just closed my eyes for a minute."

"Why?"

"To hear better."

There was a roar of laughter and the dog rose up, stretched and licked Mr Spurgeon's wrist.

Without thinking, David blurted out, "There's a dog licking your wrist, sir." Then he closed his eyes against the confusion in his mind. Was he actually still dreaming? Was he going to wake up in a minute to find everything back to normal? But David knew he had never in his life had a dream like this.

There was a shout of laughter which took a long time to stop, despite Mr Spurgeon's angry warnings. Why did I say that, thought David. He was mixing up the present with – with what? He saw Jenny looking at him fearfully and suddenly felt an urgent need to lose his temper and hit someone. Preferably Gary who had been laughing louder than anyone.

"What did you say, David?"

"I said there's a dog—" He came to an embarrassed halt, but there was no more laughter – just rising curiosity about what Mr Spurgeon was going to do to him.

"Yes. I thought you said that. So you think you're a comedian, do you?"

"No, sir."

"Then what are you?"

"I don't know, sir."

"I'll tell you what you are. You're an idiot, Golding. What are you?"

"An idiot, sir."

There was a trickle of quickly suppressed

laughter and then the silence of anticipation.

"And you know what happens to idiots, don't you, Golding?"

"No, sir." David could see the dog licking the teacher's wrist again.

"Idiots get detentions – so many detentions that they eventually have to go and see Mr Decker."

"Do they, sir?" David couldn't think of anything else to say. Besides, he was watching the dog wander slowly out of the room. As he did so, David felt a rush of normality returning, but it couldn't cancel out what had happened.

"Yes, they do. And your first one is this afternoon. For an hour."

"But—"

"Yes, David?"

"I'm sorry, sir."

"It's too late to be sorry."

David walked miserably out of detention, the grey school buildings looking shabby and gloomy in the late afternoon sun. The suburb of London they lived in was just on the edge of the Thames marshes, and although Hockley was run down and bleak, he loved it for its mysterious mists and glinting water. Now, however, he was in no mood to appreciate anything. He was hungry, the detention had seemed endless and he had loads of homework to do. But what was really making him uneasy was the see-through dog, the strange feeling of being a watcher, and the vision of Arthur, yelling at him soundlessly. What had he been trying to say so urgently?

"Oi!"

He looked up to see Jenny leaning against the scuffed bricks of the playground wall. "What are you doing here?"

"Waiting for you."

Her face told him that something else had happened.

"I saw the dog again – down by the old air raid shelter. The one that's been sealed up."

"So—?"

"He wants us to follow him."

"No way." David was adamant.

"I saw him peering out of the bike shed. He ran up to me – and then ran back to the shed again. Eventually I followed him down to those old steps and saw him disappear through the rusted-up doors."

"Disappear?" David was afraid again, and he could see that Jenny was trembling. "Do you believe in this dog, Jen?"

"Of course I do. We both saw it, didn't we." She sounded positive, but her voice shook. "I think it's a ghost."

"Ghost!" David didn't want to accept it. He

wanted to hang on to something – anything – that was rational. But what was rational? David pushed the crowding thoughts away. He just wanted to get home fast. Then with a sick feeling in the pit of his stomach he realised that at some time he would have to go to sleep – and that wasn't a nice thought at all.

"He must be – if we can see through him," Jenny was saying. "Mustn't he?" For the first time in years she was actually appealing to him.

"Er—"

"Come on." She was desperate to share the extraordinary idea with him. "He must be a ghost."

"OK, so he's a ghost." He found it better to admit the thought; but as he did so a clear, logical voice rang out in his head: Ghost? I've never believed in ghosts. Well – he did now. Then his mind raced ahead. "Arthur. You saw him too, didn't you?"

"Yes," she replied hesitantly. "I saw him. He was shouting."

"But where from?"

"He was standing on some steps."

"What were they like?" David persisted.

"Weed covered. Overgrown."

"Cracked?"

"Yes. Yes, I think so." She was staring at him, for once hanging on his every word.

"You know where those steps are, don't you?"

She nodded. "They're the steps down to the old air raid shelter."

"What are we going to do?" asked David. They stared at each other helplessly. Fear of the unknown was engulfing them, and although they both knew what they had to do, neither of them wanted to do it.

"Come on then," David said at last. "We can't just ignore it. For some reason, this is meant for us!"

That was the worst thing about it.

They walked slowly round the back of the bike shed and down the steps to the boiler house. Beyond it were more steps, cracked, overgrown, covered in weeds, protected by a barrier and a notice saying STRICTLY OUT OF BOUNDS TO ALL PUPILS. At the bottom were two rusting iron doors. There was no sign of the dog.

With some relief, David and Jenny began to walk away from the barrier, but they had not gone far when a chill feeling of foreboding swept over them and they instinctively turned round. The dog was loping silently towards them.

CHAPTER TWO

The ghost dog stopped, stared up at them and wagged his tail before running down the overgrown steps. At the bottom he stopped, snuffled, and then walked straight through one of the rusting doors. The twins stared after him, then gazed uncertainly at each other.

"Let's go home," said Jenny. "Forget it all."

"No," replied David. "We can't do that."

"Why not?"

"He came for us, didn't he? If we don't follow him now he'll come for us again – maybe at home next time."

"You mean – he might come at night?"

"He might."

"But he wants us to follow him down there." She shuddered. "We're not allowed, and besides – it's not been used in years and years. It'll be full of the most awful creepy-crawlies – and other things!"

David knew what she meant – other things like Arthur. But he was sure they had to go through with it. "We mustn't chicken out," he mumbled, wishing he'd kept his mouth shut.

"All right." Jenny pulled herself together. "We'll follow him but we need a torch."

"I've got one in my saddlebag," he acknowledged unwillingly. "I'll go and get it."

When David returned, Jenny was pushing at one of the rusting doors. It suddenly yielded, its jagged base grinding harshly on the broken concrete. She jumped back, trembling, and slowly, reluctantly, they both peered into the darkness beyond.

"Where's the dog?" David asked.

"Must be still in there."

"Let's go then. But we'll have to be quick; there's not much power left in this battery."

Making sure they were unobserved, the twins hurried into the air raid shelter, but came to a halt almost immediately. There was a musty, shut-in smell and the darkness was so intense they couldn't see a thing.

"Where's that torch?" hissed Jenny.

David waved the pale beam around but it was weak.

"That's no good," she said.

"It's all we've got. Hang on – this sometimes helps." He thumped the top of the torch and it flickered into a brighter if more erratic beam.

Jenny suddenly let out a cry of alarm. "Something touched me," she shrieked.

"Keep quiet. If we're found in here, there'll be big trouble."

"It was wet and cold."

"Yes, it's the dog's nose," pointed out David, his voice shaking. "He's trying to tell us something."

"Tell us what?"

"Or maybe lead us somewhere—"

That seemed to be more likely, for David now felt the wet nose nuzzling urgently at him. He flashed the torch around and the beam was just strong enough to illuminate what appeared to be the entrances to two tunnels.

"Do you think the shelter's circular?" he asked. "I mean, just one tunnel going round on itself."

"There's the dog's tail," whispered Jenny weakly. "This is so horrible."

"Then let's do what you said – and go home." Now it was David's turn to want to back out. The smell was making him feel sick.

"No," said Jenny. "We've got to follow him. You're right – if we don't he'll never leave us alone."

Terrified, the twins entered the right-hand tunnel, the weak beam picking up old packing cases, partly dismembered bicycles and a sewing machine. But they didn't see some mouldering car tyres and both tripped over them. It was all very well for that dog, thought David; he just goes straight through obstacles. They couldn't.

The tunnel sloped downwards, and as it did so the smell became worse, a mixture of damp earth and rotting – rotting what, Jenny wondered. Horrible images kept filling her mind and she fought back the panic that was threatening to engulf her. Rotting clothes? Rotting rats or mice? Rotting corpses? Well, there might be some clothes, she told herself, for the shelter seemed to have been used as a dump, and there could be rats or mice, but surely there wouldn't be any corpses. Determined not to lose control she slowly edged forward, but when she touched something softly fluttering in the darkness, she screamed, the hollow cry echoing down the passage beyond.

"It's only a bat," said David, sweeping the torch up to the cobweb-hung ceiling. "Look – there's dozens of them." There were, hanging upside-down, a grey mass of furry bodies and wings. Some of them were moving slightly.

"Take the light off them," said Jenny hurriedly. "We don't want to disturb any more."

David shuddered. It would be terrible to feel a small, furry, mouse-like body moving across his cheek. Then he did – or thought he did – and it was his turn to give a piercing yell.

"Be quiet," said Jenny. "We'll be heard outside."

"I couldn't help it," he protested. "Like you couldn't help it."

"Let's keep moving; it can't be much longer, can it?"

"Look," said David. "There are bench seats along the walls. People must have sat on either side, facing each other, listening to the bombs falling."

A particularly large black spider scuttled across one of the benches. David swung the beam abruptly away and they hurried on.

"The tunnel's broadening out," said David. "And I can see the dog."

"What's he doing?"

"Digging – or pulling – at something."

"Let's go faster," said Jenny. "I'm sure your rotten torch is going to give out."

The beam was getting weaker, but the twins had reached the end of the tunnel and found themselves standing in a large rectangular area, the roof held up by wooden props. Even in the fading light they could see that David had been right and the tunnel doubled back on itself towards the entrance. There were more benches, a few broken chairs and tables and the remains of an old piano. At the back were a pile of sandbags, a chipped marble table, a stove, some cabinets, and a couple of large steel drums.

"Maybe they were used to store water," suggested David, watching the dog nuzzling at the sandbags. It turned back towards the twins with an excited yelp, but the torch beam was very faint now and both David and Jenny knew that they must start on their return journey.

Directly the Labrador realised the twins were trying to get past him, it began to growl.

"Get out of the way," yelled David with sudden, unexpected aggression.

The Labrador showed no signs of moving and continued to growl menacingly.

"Get out of the way!"

"He's still trying to show us something."

"Yeah," replied David. "But it's something we can't see." The torch beam was only a pin prick now. "Let's run back," hissed David. "Don't be afraid. He's only a ghost dog after all."

As the twins pushed their way through the dog's see-through body they could feel a dense freezing cold mass. Then he sprang on them from behind, determined that they shouldn't leave.

"Let's get up the tunnel," said David. "Fast!" Both twins were terrified that they were going to be left in the dark, but so far the beam still played faintly on the mouldy damp of the brick walls.

They ran on towards the exit tunnel, only to find that it was cluttered with even more rubbish and they had to clamber over a couple of old prams as well as what looked like a wardrobe. The dog followed, growling angrily.

"Don't push!" David was trying to clamber over an old mattress, the springs of which snaked out like coiled traps in the darkness.

"The dog was trying to show us something – I'm sure of that," panted Jenny.

"Yeah," replied David unhappily. "But we've got to get out of here before this battery packs up."

As he spoke the torch went out.

CHAPTER THREE

David and Jenny were plunged into pitch darkness and the dog gave a mournful howl. The twins stood there, conscious of the silence creeping over them like a soft blanket full of spiders.

David gave out a little whinny of fear. "Something touched my feet," he stuttered. "Something soft and scuttling. Maybe it was a rat."

"Try the torch again."

"It's dead." He snapped the switch again and again, but there was not the slightest chink of light. "We'll have to chance our luck. It can't be that far back."

"I hope this tunnel does go back to the entrance." Jenny was losing her nerve. She shuddered.

"Now what?"

"There's something in my hair. Something running." Jenny gave a sob of despair. "It's horrible – suppose this tunnel is taking us *away* from the entrance."

"Where else could it go?"

"I don't know—"

"Where?" he persisted.

"Shut up, David."

"Grab my T-shirt and we'll move on together."

Then they both felt the dog pushing its way through. For once, his presence seemed almost reassuring.

"Maybe he'll lead us out," said Jenny hopefully.

"I think it's running away," replied David pessimistically.

But it wasn't. The dog stayed a few metres ahead, turning occasionally to give a yelp. Although the twins still managed to fall over another mattress, something that felt like a tandem, and what Jenny thought was a chest of drawers, they finally fought their way back to the rusty doors. One of them was still standing half open, letting in rich evening sunlight, a welcome sight after their long dark stumbling journey.

Then someone stepped into the sunlight – and out of it again. The twins stood stock-still, knowing they had been discovered. If it was Len, the school caretaker, they would probably be suspended, for he rightly clamped down hard on any pupils trespassing in the shelter. But it wasn't the caretaker. It was someone dressed in the most extraordinary and unfamiliar clothes. At the same time, although they could still see the bright sunlight, the atmosphere became bitterly cold.

The dog bounded towards the figure with a bark of delight, and the large man with a bushy black moustache, shiny suit and trilby hat knelt down and opened his arms to the Labrador. As he did so, the chill seemed to penetrate deep into their bones, making it difficult to breathe.

"That's Arthur," whispered David. "Don't you recognise him from the photographs?"

"Yes," replied Jenny. "But what on earth is he doing down here?"

Arthur stood up, stretched, looked right through them and then, whistling to the dog, began to walk down the tunnel. He showed not the slightest sign of being aware of them. Gradually, as he disappeared so did the numbing cold and the twins felt the heady warmth of dappled sunlight.

David and Jenny stood outside, feeling shaky and uncertain. Compared to the menacing aura of Arthur, the dog had seemed positively friendly. It was hard to remember that Arthur had a good side. He might have been very generous to the Animal Sanctuary all those years ago, but what did he want with them? And what had the dog been trying to show them?

"Only the dog can see us," said David. "I'm sure Arthur can't."

"But why can the dog? I didn't know dead Labradors were psychic."

"They're not," said David. "At least, not as far as I know. But we can see him for a reason – and that reason's connected with the furthest part of the shelter, down by the sandbags. That dog's come back to try and show us something – and I'm sure it's connected with Arthur."

"Do you know how he died?" Jenny asked.

"Haven't a clue. I just know he died in the war. Mum and Dad must know."

"Maybe they do," said Jenny doubtfully, "but I'm not sure whether they'll tell us."

"Why not?" David was impatient. "What have they got to hide?"

"He was a crook, wasn't he?"

"So?"

"Maybe he died doing something crooked." Jenny looked cautiously around her and closed the door of the air raid shelter with tremendous relief. But she knew it was only a temporary reprieve; the dark tunnels had not finished with them yet.

Their mother was furious about the detention.

"It wasn't my fault, Mum," protested David, knowing that he could hardly tell her – or Dad – about the dog or even Arthur. They would think he'd gone crazy.

Susan Golding was an outspoken woman, a driving force in the family. She worked for an estate agent, a job she hated but handled with her usual efficiency. She even found time to help her husband with his small building business which had hit hard times. The Goldings lived on a housing estate in Hockley near the Thames.

"Mr Spurgeon said you were asleep in class."

"I was knackered, Mum."

"Yes – watching TV till all hours. If this happens again I'm going to have that set taken out of your room. It was a mistake in the first place, if you ask me. Just wait till your dad comes home—" She was crashing around so much serving their tea that it was a wonder she didn't hurl David's burger and beans straight at him.

"Mum—" Jenny knew it wasn't the best time to ask her mother about Arthur, but she was consumed with curiosity. "You know that project about families Mrs Spinner has asked us to do—"

"Well?"

"Suppose I wrote about your Great Uncle Arthur?"

"What?" Her mother was poised with the bread knife. "What did you say?"

"Suppose I wrote about Arthur," she repeated.

"Are you insane?"

"I only—"

"That crook!"

"He was your great uncle," put in David with an incredible lack of tact. Jenny scowled at him.

"Exactly. That's why I keep him hushed up. Do you think I'm proud of him? Do you think I want him written up for a school project?" But she paused, teapot in hand, and now there was a softer, reflective look on her face. "Not that he was all bad – you've got to realise that. OK, he was a villain and he stole a lot of money, but he gave it away, you know. And then when he came out of the nick – prison I mean – he went straight for a while and built up a nice little business."

"What kind of business?"

"Fish. Wet fish. Used to have a shop and a delivery van. Went right down to Whitstable to pick up some of the catch – ever so fresh it was. Then he sold the shop and the van for a profit – and gave it all to the Animal Sanctuary. Loved animals he did – especially dogs. Always had the same kind of Labrador – always called them Bert. And he was good to Mum. Used to give her pocket money. Of course Arthur could please himself in the war and he certainly didn't miss an opportunity. He couldn't join up or even have a reserved occupation because of his heart condition." Their mother was smiling now, still holding the teapot and remembering her mother's stories with happy nostalgia. Of course, David had to spoil it all.

"Wonder where the money to set up the business came from?" he asked.

"What was that?" she said vaguely, not really connecting with the present. Jenny wondered if she was sufficiently connected with the teapot.

"Was Arthur married?" she asked, but that wasn't the right question either and Susan Golding frowned. "He was, but he was never faithful – except to his Berts. Anyway – he died young," she added conclusively, implying that Arthur had been snuffed out by some God-given act of justice.

"How did he die?" asked Jenny hesitantly, knowing she had arrived at the crucial bit. "Was it his heart?"

Their mother paused. "As a matter of fact it was in that old air raid shelter in your school."

"Blimey," said David. "Why didn't you tell us before?"

"Because I didn't want to. It was morbid and I thought you might be frightened. I wish they'd get rid of that place. It's dangerous like that – all boarded up." She glared fiercely at both of them. "If I ever thought you'd go in there—"

"Of course we wouldn't," said David, helpful at last. "It's out of bounds. And besides, I'm scared of the dark."

"Are you?" said his mother and Jenny winced, knowing her twin had gone too far as usual. "Now when did that come on?"

David was flustered. "I don't know. It's been coming on for some time. Don't know why really. I—"

"You said Arthur died in the shelter?" interrupted Jenny. "Was it during an air raid?"

"No—" Susan Golding was hesitant. Then she hurried on, knowing she couldn't stop now. Her twins were far too persistent for that. "He was found in there. He'd had a heart attack of course. I think it was right at the end of the war. Anyway, Bert – one of the Berts – was with him."

"How sad," said Jenny.

"It was." Susan Golding sighed. "My mum was very fond of her uncle. But of course he'd slipped back to a life of crime—" She paused. "Now listen, Jenny, I want you to make me a promise. I don't want him written up, right? Anyone else in the family – but not him."

"I promise, Mum." She winked at David as her mother turned back to the stove. At least they had the information they had wanted. But what did it mean? And would the ghosts of the past appear again? Jenny had been praying that Arthur and his dog wouldn't bother them anymore, but she was sure they would – and she knew instinctively her twin was thinking the same.

CHAPTER FOUR

"No," said Elsie Styles. "You don't get no more chips."

David was standing by the canteen counter with his best friend Tim.

"Please," said Tim. "Go on, Elsie. I can hardly see any on this plate."

"I could count my chips on the fingers of one hand," moaned David. "We'll starve to death."

Elsie put her hands on her vast hips as she glared at the two boys. Her elaborately tinted hairstyle stood on end and her many chins wobbled angrily. She was a character, much loved, but she also had a temper.

"Listen, you two. We're economising."

"Since when?" asked Tim. He was short and stocky and his mother had told him not to eat chips anyway but to go for the healthy diet end of the canteen. But Tim preferred chips – not "rabbit food" as he called the salad bar – and he was prepared to make an issue of it.

"Go on, Elsie. Give us a double. I'll be your mate for life."

To David's annoyance, Tim was using all his

considerable charm which was too often irritatingly successful.

"It's the school disco tonight, Elsie. You're coming, aren't you? I'll give you a good time. You see if I don't. But I'll need the chips."

Elsie suddenly grinned. "I'll be serving up food tonight – like I'm always doing. You won't see me on the floor."

"Want to make a bet?"

"Get on with it," said Tracy-Ann, coming up behind them. "What are you doing? Chatting our Elsie up?"

"Sort of," said Tim. "Come on, Else. Do us a favour."

"Push off, you two," she said, dumping more chips on their plates. "And less of your lip!"

As she shovelled on the last chip, David felt the cold coming like a great cloud rushing towards him. He couldn't see it but he knew exactly what it meant – Bert. His heart began to beat faster, his mouth dry. The very thought of eating those chips was nauseating. He scanned the room and saw Jenny at a nearby table. She seemed transfixed. Her friends were gazing at her curiously, but David knew she too had sensed Bert's chilling presence. He shivered. Once again he had the feeling that he had become a spectator to the scene that he was actually in.

A scream suddenly cut through the normal hubbub of the canteen. Elsie's companion, a little old lady called Winnie who was serving up wizened sausages, screamed and screamed again. At first, the long line of pupils hadn't the slightest idea what she was screaming about. But when David saw Bert with the sausages dangling from his mouth that he knew that the ghost dog was either hungry, or, more likely, in the habit of being hungry.

"Them bangers," said Tracy-Ann. "They're floating in the air, like."

"Must be hot air rising." Jon Blake wanted to be a scientist. "In some way or the other," he added hastily in case anyone started to cross-examine him.

"There goes a meat pie," said Tracy-Ann, and Winnie immediately had a fit of hysterics.

A nervous cheer came from a group of boys as the pie spun round the canteen, joining the sausages that were now slithering across the floor.

"There goes a doughnut," said Tim, looking scared now.

Then it was the turn of another and another until Mr Spurgeon hurried across to the canteen counter and everyone fell silent. He spluttered, stared around him accusingly, and then shouted, "Who is responsible for this – this outrage? Come on, I want the culprit to own up. What sort of stupid trick do you think you're playing? I don't know how this is done but—" He broke off abruptly, and they all stared in amazement at the final doughnut rising from its tray and then flying back towards Mr Spurgeon. It landed at his feet and splattered jam all over the floor. "Who did this?" he gibbered. "Who is responsible? Was it you, Henderson?" He glared at a boy on a nearby table who had started laughing uncontrollably.

Maybe he was just hysterical, like Winnie, thought Jenny. Most of the pupils in the dining hall had been too overawed by the incredible situation to say much. Dougie Henderson had been one of the few who had lost control.

"It's nothing to do with me, sir," Dougie protested, but he looked guilty and Mr Spurgeon began to stride towards him.

"Stop laughing, boy. Stop laughing now. If you've got anything to do with—"

He had overlooked the fact that the jammy contents of the doughnut were now slowly spreading across the floor in a crimson lake. Mr Spurgeon skidded, waved his arms desperately, skidded again and then went down with a tremendous thump. He lay there groaning as Winnie's screams grew even louder.

The strawberry jam was all over Mr Spurgeon's chest and hands, and as he rose shakily to his feet, apparently dripping in gore, Winnie's worst fears were confirmed and she had to be led away by Elsie.

"I'm going straight to the Head," Mr Spurgeon said furiously. "He'll institute an enquiry. Whoever was responsible will of course be banned from tonight's disco."

As Mr Spurgeon strode towards the doors, Bert trotted up to Jenny and sat down beside her. David hurried over, wanting to protect her but feeling more terrified than ever. If Bert could create this kind of chaos, then he must be very powerful indeed, and if he was that powerful, then they had no chance of resisting his will.

The coldness began to disperse and David saw that the ghost dog was fading. Had Bert come to demonstrate his strength? To warn them that they had to obey him? With a sinking heart David knew that he had.

CHAPTER FIVE

The school's PA system thundered out heavy metal in a hall that was decorated with rather tattered bunting. The stage was stacked with disco equipment and the floor was crowded with wildly gyrating pupils, some of whom were taking up more space than others as they showed off to their friends. Various teachers stood around like vigilantes, alert for the slightest hint of a problem. The Head Teacher, Philip Decker, who prided himself on not being stuffy, danced an embarrassingly old-fashioned jive with Angela Horrocks, one of the PE instructors. As usual, the school disco was its completely naff self.

Mr Decker had read the whole school a lecture at an extra assembly about being "disruptive" in the canteen, and had managed to get round the flying food by talking about the "strange, inexplicable phenomena" that he was still "looking into".

David and Jenny hadn't had a chance for a private talk until now, because they had gone home from school with different friends. At tea, Mum had read them a long lecture about how to behave at the disco and about being ready when their father came to pick them up. When they were dressed their father had driven them back to the school with warnings of his own.

David was wearing his best jeans and a baggy sweater and Jenny wore her new mini-skirt with a skinny top. They had been looking forward to the disco, but since the appearance of Bert and Arthur it had paled into insignificance.

"We've got to find out what Bert wants," said Jenny. "And why we can see him when no one else can."

"And why has he singled us out?" complained David.

"Because we're family," she replied. "It must be family business."

The disco ground to a halt as the Head Teacher mounted the stage dressed in a velvet jacket, drainpipe trousers and a red bow tie that looked as if it ought to light up and whirl round.

"Ladies and gentlemen, boys and girls." Mr Decker smiled patronisingly, clasping and unclasping his hands as he always did when he spoke in public. "As you may know, the proceeds of this year's disco – as well as the raffle – are going to our local Animal Sanctuary which was established as far back as 1935 and has been open ever since. It does wonderful work, but now the Sanctuary may have to close, which will not just be sad for us after all the support we've given it, but for all the stray animals in the streets as well as the ones that are badly treated at home or elsewhere. Now I'm going to introduce Gillian Cole who, as many of you will know, is the director of the Sanctuary." Mr Decker gave her a courtly little half bow as she mounted the steps to a patter of applause.

Gillian Cole was young and had a no-nonsense attitude that made Mr Decker look uneasy – as if she was upstaging him. "I'm sorry to interrupt this disco, but we're pretty desperate at the Sanctuary right now and only have funds left for another couple of weeks at most. I think the majority of you will know where we are – on the site of the old bus depot. It's not much to look at but we've pulled off some pretty terrific rescues recently, and if we can't pay the rent an awful lot of animals will have to be put down. At the moment we've got four donkeys, five goats and a whole litter of pigs as well as the usual neglected or abandoned domestic animals. Only last Monday we managed to rescue a couple of pet rabbits reduced to skin and bone. On Tuesday we found a Labrador puppy roaming the streets – beautiful dog. It had been turned out by a family who simply didn't want him any longer. So please, everyone – give as generously as you can. Save the Sanctuary. Keep our animals from being destroyed."

"Thank you. Thank you," Mr Decker got in before she could receive too much applause. "I know everyone will give generously. This school has, I'm proud to say, a history of generous—"

"I feel cold," said Jenny apprehensively. "Really cold. I think something's going to happen."

"So do I," whispered David. "And I know why. Look over there. The ghost dog's back."

Bert was half in and half out of the door. Then he disappeared – only to return almost immediately.

"He wants us to follow him," said Jenny uncertainly.

"It had to come sooner or later." David made up his mind suddenly. "Let's get it over with."

"Now?"

"Yes. Now."

The air raid siren started as a slow distant wail and then became louder. At first Jenny thought it came from the disco, that it was the beginning of a new sound she hadn't heard before. There was also a sort of rattling bell which came and went from outside. Then she saw the warden with a tin helmet bustling into the hall. The bone-piercing cold spread inside her as the dancers faded, their bodies becoming more and more insubstantial every moment. This was worse than before. It was as if they were being swallowed up by the past.

"David!" She couldn't even see her twin now. "David," she called, panic making her turn this way and that, her mind racing.

"I'm here."

"Where?"

"Here Jenny. But where are you? Jenny! Jenny! I can't see anything. I can't see you." He felt like a frightened child again, calling out in the night, full of nameless and shifting fears. He too had seen the warden and now the dancers were see-through – like Bert. Shadows jumped and merged; he suddenly realised that unfamiliar grey shirts and shorts and blazers and jumpers and skirts and polished black shoes were everywhere. The clothes were very different to their own and the boys had plastered-down hair that made their ears stick out on either side.

At last he saw Jenny and she saw him. They clung to each other in the swirling movement, the only substantial figures in a world that had lost all sense and meaning. The cold air rose and seemed to blast into their faces, searing their skin. Then the pain decreased and they both felt nothing at all; it was as if their bodies were light and floating. And their fear was intense.

"Children—"

Suddenly, the scene sharpened and David muttered, "I don't believe it."

"Where are we?" hissed Jenny.

"Still in the school. It's the same hall but it's – different."

"I don't get you."

"Neither do I," admitted David.

"Children!" Again the light sharpened and now they could see a couple of hundred pupils standing in the hall, clutching boxes – boxes that looked ominous.

"What are they carrying?" asked David.

"Gas masks. Think back and remember that project we did on the war. Those are gas masks all right."

"Where are we?"

"Somewhere in the past, I think," Jenny replied. "In wartime." The siren continued to wail. The children around them were putting down the gas mask boxes and struggling into their dark blue macs.

"Children."

The woman was standing on the stage, her hair in a bun. Her tweed suit, her sensible stockings and shoes were so different from the way their teachers dressed that the twins regarded her as some kind of alien creature from an old film on Sunday afternoons. Then David remembered who she was. "That's Miss Perry," he said. "She was in the project too. The photographs made her look a right old bat, but she's not like that now, is she? Her face is kind." He was desperate for at least one benign adult in this dreadful past that had sucked them in so quickly.

Would they ever get back to their own time, Jenny wondered, looking round her and seeing the misty, insubstantial room beginning to have hard edges, to take on a more positive shape.

"Everyone listen." Miss Perry was standing on a platform in a different part of the hall from the stage. Behind her was a photograph of King George VI and a flag – the Union Jack. Around the dark panelled walls were pictures of past Head Teachers and a large sign read *WATCH AND PRAY.* "That's the air raid siren," said Miss Perry. "But, as usual, there's nothing to worry about. In a few moments we're going to be walking slowly and in a very orderly way out of the hall, across the playground and into the shelter where we're all going to be absolutely safe – as we always are."

The hall was growing more distinct by the second and Jenny could see the teachers standing round the edge of the room. There was a large clock she had never seen before which made a loud rhythmic ticking. Sweat broke out on her forehead.

"You know what I'm thinking?" she whispered urgently.

"Yeah—" David's voice trembled. Then he pulled himself together. "But we're not."

"Not?"

"Trapped in time."

At moments of high stress, the twins always seemed to be able to read each other's minds – and they had never had a more stressful moment than this.

"It's temporary," said David, but he sounded more hopeful than certain.

"How temporary?"

"It must be something to do with Bert. We know he wanted us to follow him back in time – to when he was alive – so this must be Arthur's and Bert's time, mustn't it?"

Jenny nodded, but the idea didn't in any way lessen her fears. She was now sure they were trapped in the past and she even remembered Mr Decker with affection. Only Bert held the key to their escape; at least, she hoped he did.

Then another thought occurred to her. "Can any of them see us?" asked Jenny.

David shook his head. "I'm sure they can't. I mean – if they could they'd have made a fuss. We're dressed a bit differently to them for a start, aren't we?"

The last of the children were filing out now and Jenny saw Miss Perry walking sedately behind them, handbag in one hand and gas mask in the other. She looked calm; there was something deeply reassuring about her – and not just to her own pupils. Jenny took some heart. If Arthur turned out to be as sinister as he had previously appeared, then maybe they could turn to Miss Perry. But then she realised with a deadening certainty that there was no way Miss Perry could ever help. Their lives were running parallel but would never touch. She and David were on their own.

"We'd better go with them," said David. "Down into the shelter. I think that's the only way out."

"Out?" Jenny gazed at him in horror. "Go down there to get out. Are you crazy?"

"Bert needs us," he said hopelessly.

"We don't need him," replied Jenny fervently.

"No, but he's not going to release us, is he? Unless we do what he wants."

"We'll be trapped – with Arthur."

"I'm sure it's our only way back," said David woodenly.

Jenny suddenly knew her twin was right. But she wished he wasn't.

The twins followed Miss Perry and the children out into the playground which was surrounded by unfamiliar high railings and had outside toilets. It was summer and the sun was high in an innocent sky. The playground gate was open and a constant stream of people were beginning to form a crowd, the men in hats, the women in headscarves, all hurrying towards the shelter, but standing back for the crocodile of children to go in first.

Then the twins saw they were all looking into the sky, and when they gazed up too, David and Jenny could see a black speck, going straight overhead with a stuttering drone.

"Buzz bomb," said someone in the crowd. "It seems to be passing over us."

There was a barrage balloon floating nearby and the twins heard a young man say, "Let's hope it don't hit the cables – or there'll be one hell of a bang."

"Wasn't the school bombed?" whispered David.

"I can't remember. I think some of it was."

"Maybe this is the day it happened," he said frantically.

"Let's get inside," she snapped. "It doesn't matter what day it is."

"We can't be hurt." David tried to reassure her. "We're not really here."

"I wouldn't be so sure," said Jenny, hurrying after Miss Perry's retreating back. "Depends how deeply we're in the past."

"But we'd alter history," continued David.

"Shut up!" she snapped. "Shut up and get in the shelter."

★

Despite the menacing presence of the doodlebug, the entry into the air raid shelter was orderly, supervised by the warden they had seen in the school hall and a woman in the same uniform. The line seemed endless, but there was no panic as David and Jenny climbed down the steps and into the reception area just in front of the two tunnels. There was an old school desk and behind this was another warden, sitting on a battered chair, writing up some kind of report form.

David shivered as he walked past him. The warden was elderly and would have been dead for many years in the twins' own time. He suddenly remembered the cemetery at Hockley. If they hadn't been cremated, many of the people in the shelter would be there in their graves.

As they walked down the first tunnel, the twins discovered it was clean and well-scrubbed, giving off a strong aroma of disinfectant. The benches were freshly painted and had long home-made cushions. The outline of the walls and objects was even sharper now, but there was still a slight furring at the edges, a minute shifting that made them realise that time was still playing with them. But at least the rigours of the blasting chill had not returned.

There were a number of warning notices on the walls about keeping a full blackout at the windows and a very large one that said: CARELESS TALK

COSTS LIVES. The twins could also hear the hissing of tea urns further up the shelter and knew it was the reality of the scene that made them both so afraid.

Eventually, David and Jenny found a couple of spare places and sat down, only to have two women almost immediately sitting on their laps – except "sitting" was definitely the wrong word to use. The twins both felt as if they had been touched by a soft feather, and after that there was no sensation at all. They could see through the two women, but they could also hear them talking about last night's raid. It was a horrible feeling, thought Jenny, as if she and David were in some way temporarily inhabiting their bodies.

Then Arthur appeared, pushing a trolley loaded with tea and buns. He was wearing his usual shiny suit, trilby hat and a tie with too many stripes.

The smile on his face seemed sinister.

"Do you think he realises we're here?" whispered Jenny urgently.

"Who knows?" replied David.

There was a delighted yelp and Jenny could feel Bert licking her ankle. He could certainly see them.

"Hello, Arthur," said a man on the opposite bench. "How's the world treating you then?"

"All right. Can't grumble." His voice was hoarse and deep.

"Good to see you dishing out the Rosie Lee."

"Got to do me bit, haven't I?"

"Hear you sold the shop."

"And the van. Clean break."

"What's all this about giving the profits to that place for stray animals."

"I gave them something."

"Not like you."

"Eh?"

"Giving money away." The man laughed to take the sting out of his words but David had the feeling that there was more to it than that, that he was almost cross-examining Arthur, and that Arthur didn't like it one bit. He tried to push forward with the trolley, but his way was blocked by a stout woman with two shopping bags who was having a long gossip with a friend. "Not like you, Arthur," repeated the man.

"Excuse me, madam."

But the stout lady didn't hear him and Arthur was trapped with his interrogator.

"Nasty business about Barclays," the man said pointedly, his eyes never leaving Arthur's face.

"Eh?"

"Talk about taking advantage of an air raid."

"What's all this?" Arthur was brusque.

"You mean you didn't hear about the hold-up at Barclays Bank yesterday – during the raid. Where've you been?"

"Slipped down to see me sister-in-law in Margate."

"Yeah – come to think of it, didn't see you in here yesterday."

"No." Arthur pushed the trolley at the woman's back. "Clear the way, please." But she still didn't hear and he said reluctantly, "What happened at Barclays then?"

"Masked gunman walks straight in and asks for all they got."

"What did they do?"

"Gave it to him, of course. When the bombs are about to drop you don't hang around to argue with a gun, do you?" There was a slightly mocking note to the man's voice now – or was it just her imagination, wondered Jenny.

"Not likely."

"Walked out – got clean away. But I was talking to Inspector Wren."

"Oh yes?" Arthur was definitely acting casual.

"You know Inspector Wren, don't you?"

"Slightly."

"He reckons it's a local job and the loot's still around somewhere."

"Oh yes?"

"What do you reckon, Arthur?"

"No idea, Ron." He called him by his name for the first time. "How's the wounded foot?"

"Giving me gip."

"Reckon it'll keep you out of the action?"

"For a long time, Arthur. For a very long time."

"Didn't shoot yourself in that foot, did you, Ron?'

"What an idea, Arthur. What an idea." Ron laughed uneasily.

Arthur barged the trolley at the stout woman's considerable backside and she bounded forward with an angry exclamation. "Mind your backs, please." He pushed his trolley on down the tunnel.

"Be seeing you, Arthur."

"See you, Ron."

Now the trolley had gone, David and Jenny could see Arthur's inquisitor. Ron was a tall man with a long, lean, craggy face, clean-shaven with dark penetrating eyes. He was leaning heavily on a walking stick and watching Arthur's back with considerable distaste.

CHAPTER SIX

A stuttering drone began above the shelter and there was a sudden silence as everyone looked up at the ceiling in foreboding.

"Buzz bomb – doodlebug," said the stout woman, a kind of frightened excitement in her voice. "Sounds like a plane and then the fuel cuts out; falls out of the sky. Without a sound."

There was an electrifying hush. David and Jenny held their breath. The silence seemed to go on forever – until an explosion rocked the shelter. Dust fell and Jenny was sure one of the struts that held up the ceiling shook slightly. Ron's eyes were dilated with fear, the stout woman was trembling, a child began to cry, and then someone started to sing. The twins had heard the song before. It had never held any particular significance for them, but down here it was so haunting, so moving that they were both close to tears.

We'll meet again, don't know where, don't know when,
But I know we'll meet again some sunny day . . .

For some strange reason, David and Jenny felt the words held a meaning especially for them. They felt cheered but more than that; the song seemed to have given them strength.

"That was close," Ron said to the stout lady as the singing died away.

"If it's got your number on it—" she replied gloomily.

"Hang on – here come the coppers. Now I wonder what they want down here."

"Inspector Wren," Ron said with artificial warmth.

"Hello, my old china." The policeman was tall and almost as wide, with a military moustache rather like Arthur's. He was followed by two other officers.

"What are you doing? Come to arrest Jerry, have you? You won't find him down here – only up there in the clouds." Ron chortled at his own feeble joke.

"It's 'down here' we want to have a look at," said the policeman grimly.

"Nothing to do with that bank raid, is it?" Ron asked and his large lady companion looked curious, despite the noise of another bomb exploding close by and the shelter shaking much harder than before.

"You mind your business – and I'll mind mine."

"Arthur's on the tea trolley," said Ron quickly. "Get yourself a cuppa down the other end."

"That would be nice," said the policeman. "Good old Arthur. Always does his bit, doesn't he?"

"He certainly does," agreed Ron enthusiastically.

"Gave a handy sum to the Animal Sanctuary, didn't he?"

"He certainly did."

There was a long pause. Then as he moved on the policeman said, "Be seeing you, Ron."

It seemed to Jenny as though there was some conspiracy between the two men.

"Ron looks a right grass, doesn't he?" said David. "Do you reckon the police suspect Arthur of being the bank robber?"

"I get that impression," said Jenny.

"And Ron?"

"I've got really bad feelings about him," she replied, the strength of the song still supporting her.

Five minutes later, the all-clear siren sounded and people started to get up and file out.

"We'll have to stick around," said Jenny quietly.

"What for?" David said anxiously.

"See what Arthur's up to. Bert wants us here."

"Maybe he's not up to anything at all," said David defensively. He had that vacant expression that Jenny associated with his bouts of acute home-sickness – an expression she remembered seeing at school camp last year. For him, the strength was already running out.

"I think we should take a look," she said firmly.

"Do you think Bert will let us go soon?" David asked.

"Only when we've done what he wants."

Ron and the stout woman got to their feet and began to walk away, and a few minutes later there was no one left in the shelter. Jenny had a tight feeling inside and knew that her strength was running out too. Were they going to be condemned to wander forever through the corridors of the past? Just be shadows that other people sat on? They heard the sound of barking and panting – and Bert ran up to them, wagging his tail and putting his paws on their knees.

"If anyone's going to help us," said David, trying to sound positive, "it's going to be Bert."

Jenny looked into the big brown eyes of the Labrador as it panted away in front of her. "I can trust you, can't I?" she pleaded, but Bert was already moving away. Now that he was back in his own time, he seemed much friendlier and certainly warmer.

"What about the police?" asked David. But he wasn't really worried about the police; they belonged to the past. Bert was nuzzling at him now, walking off a few steps and then coming back and nuzzling again. Clearly he wanted the twins to follow him.

"Maybe he'll lead us out – and back to the disco," David said hopefully.

"He's going the other way," replied Jenny bleakly.

The twins followed Bert to the end of the tunnel and into the big space that lay beyond. It was almost cosy. There were tables and chairs, a bookcase full of thrillers and detective stories and an old Calor gas stove. Shelves held pots and pans and there was even an old Welsh dresser as well as a threadbare carpet on the floor. The piano that they had seen so many years later was at an angle to the wall and its black surface shone with polish.

The other part of the tunnel opened darkly, but opposite a pile of sandbags rose up against the wall. There was no one around, just an eerie silence – the sort of silence a room has after a number of people have left. A kind of resettling.

A radio stood on the wooden dresser and by it a half drunk cup of tea. They heard someone moving.

CHAPTER SEVEN

Cautiously, the twins went up to the wall of sandbags. They were piled about six deep and it was obvious that this was a store of spares as there were spaces where some had been removed and others were dumped into a wheelbarrow.

Jenny was the first to peer round the corner, only to discover a pale electric light bulb glowing over an inner space with a telephone, and a dining-room table surrounded by six chairs. There was a filing cabinet and a desk scattered with papers about air raid alerts and various instructions from the local authority. On the dining-room table was a sign saying *COMMAND POST. DO NOT ENTER.* Kneeling on the floor and fiddling with one of the sandbags was Arthur.

Bert trotted round the corner, nuzzling at David and Jenny while his owner looked up and said quietly, "Come on, boy. Show us a bit of loving."

The Labrador went over to him, wagging his tail and licking Arthur's face.

"Good boy. It's going to be all right. You'll be OK at the Sanctuary if anything happens. I've got your place all set up and plenty of dosh – not just to pay for you but to keep them going for years and years." He was holding Bert's furry jowls in both hands, half addressing the Labrador, half thinking aloud. "If only Ron doesn't go to the police – like he's been threatening to. I'll do for him one of these days." He shivered. "Do you know, boy, I reckon someone's just walked over my grave. I've been feeling that recently – as if I'm being watched over. That's why I don't think I've got so much time left. Never mind, old friend, I've got you for a bit longer anyway. You're my mate – my only mate now." Arthur buried his face in the Labrador's furry body and the twins heard him sob. "Good old Bert – from a long line of Berts. My last Bert." Arthur then pulled himself together abruptly and stood up. "What am I doing?" he muttered to himself. "First signs of madness talking to yourself – or even your dog."

"It is the first sign of madness, Arthur." The voice seemed to come out of nowhere and there was something vaguely familiar about it. The twins turned to each other and Jenny mouthed the name. Ron. There he was, strolling out of the exit tunnel, hands in pockets, grinning. But there was tremendous hostility in the air as the two men stared at each other. Jenny and David immediately sensed the hatred between them.

"What do you want?" demanded Arthur.

"You know what I want."

Bert was stiffening now, a long, slow growl building up in his throat. He stood protectively in front of Arthur, teeth beginning to bare.

"Whatever you want – you're not getting it."

"You keep that dog under control." Ron was slightly uneasy now.

"You stay away from him then." Arthur became a little less flustered, but he was wary.

"You owe me," said Ron.

"Do I?"

"Why don't you stop playing games?" He walked a few steps towards Arthur, but Bert's growling increased.

"Hop it, Ron – before Bert gets nasty."

"Where is it?" he asked quietly.

"Where's what?"

"The money."

"I don't know about no money." Arthur was truculent.

"The money from Barclays."

"Oh that. I didn't go anywhere near the place. You got the wrong bloke."

"No I haven't, Arthur." Ron spoke slowly and menacingly. "You were the raider and I know you've got the loot. Ten grand, wasn't it? And you've got it down here somewhere. Haven't you?"

"I'd be a fool if I had," replied Arthur. "The

coppers have been down here searching haven't they?"

"You're no fool. You go for the obvious places, don't you? So obvious, they work."

Arthur laughed a booming laugh. "Don't know what you're going on about, mate."

"Remember Wandsworth. Two grand hidden under the paving stones by that bus stop in Crepley Avenue? Another two grand in the false bottom of your summer house? Need I go on?"

"That was before I reformed and gave up the bad life," laughed Arthur, his jokey tone falling horribly flat.

"I set up that warehouse job for you in Crepley. You said you'd pay me. You never did."

"Got nicked, didn't I?"

"Not before you'd salted away most of the loot. The coppers only found the tip of the iceberg, didn't they? And it's strange that when you came out you had enough capital to lease a shop and buy a van. Very strange."

"My missus financed me – from her Aunty's legacy. You know that."

"I don't know that." There was a click and something glinted in Ron's hand.

It was a knife; David and Jenny could both see it, despite the pale light. The blade was thin and cruel and sharp.

"Now, I know you've got this coronary condition, Arthur," said Ron quietly.

Jenny and David's hearts were pounding. Was this how Arthur died? Was the coronary story just a blind?

"You shouldn't be messing about thieving in your state of health. You're a delicate man."

"You come near me, Ron, and I'll set Bert on you." Arthur's voice was full of menace.

"Then Bert will end up skewered, won't he? So you keep him under control. Understand?"

"We've got to do something," said David breathlessly.

"How can we? This is the past. It can't be interfered with."

Ron was edging closer to Arthur, a tight little smile on his lips, the blade gleaming. "Come on – make it easy – all I want is what you owe me."

"Push off," said Arthur. He was calm and chillingly calculating.

"I'll go to the police. I'll tell 'em you got the loot down here. Somewhere."

"Tell them what you like. They won't find it," said Arthur confidently.

"I mean business."

"So does Bert." The Labrador was quivering now, ready to spring, and the growling was deeper and more ferocious than ever.

"I've got to do something," David whispered to Jenny again.

"You can't. It's all over. There's nothing you can do to change history, David. And if you try – think of all the complications."

"I can't just stand by and see this happen." Before Jenny could stop him, David instinctively ran forward and dived at Ron's legs. He went straight through them.

David found himself lying on the debris-strewn floor of the shelter with the smell of stale damp rising up around him. But where was Jenny? David couldn't see a thing. It was pitch black and absolutely silent in the old shelter and there was no sign of his sister. He whispered her name and then shouted, but there was no reply. David's voice sounded thin and scared and lost in the musty darkness.

"Jenny," he called. "Jenny. Where are you?"

Terrible thoughts jumbled into his head. Had the past rejected him because he'd tried to inter-fere? Was his twin locked into the past? Would he only see her as a captive ghost? Or perhaps never at all?

David's chest tightened unbearably as the horror of it all spread inside him.

All of a sudden, Jenny came staggering out of

the debris that had once been the kitchen. David leant trembling against the wall.

"Where did you come from?" he demanded angrily.

"Where did *you* go?" she retorted. Jenny's eyes were full of tears as she rushed across the space, almost tripping over a packing case. She grabbed her brother's arm. "Well?"

"I tried to interfere and suddenly I was back here. I know I shouldn't have—"

She sighed. "You always have to find out for yourself, don't you?"

"So how did you get back?"

"Same way," she admitted. "Kind of instinct, I s'pose. I grabbed at Ron – my hand went right through him and I landed back here."

"But we can still see!"

Jenny looked about her in amazement. "It's as if those lights are still on – those electric light bulbs."

There was certainly a pale glow but it was already fading. "Do you think time's being kind to us?" he asked. "For once?"

"I don't know. But we've got to move fast," said Jenny. "If we don't, then it'll be pitch dark again."

"Shouldn't we look for the money?"

"It won't still be here," said Jenny impatiently.

"Why not?"

"Arthur would have spent it – or given it away. Or maybe Ron took it."

"That means Arthur was *murdered*. Let's just look at that Command Post. We could check—"

The light was getting dimmer and he hesitated.

"Come on, David!" Jenny yelled. "We can't go back in the dark. Not again."

"Why not?"

"Anyway, you'll never be able to search without light. Let's come back with torches. Torches that work," she added.

"OK," David agreed grudgingly, following her towards the exit tunnel. "I've got a feeling we've made a mess of this."

"We've got our spirit guide – Bert – and we've seen Arthur and Ron and Miss Perry and her kids and loads of other people. We've made a start," Jenny said hopefully, but then her voice became weak. "It's not over yet though."

David stumbled on in the now rapidly fading light. "We're not hunting ghosts – just for the sake of it. We've got mixed up with them for a purpose. I mean, Bert didn't come back for us for nothing. So there will be an end to it all."

"You're right." Now they were half-way up the tunnel Jenny was feeling better and more able to think straight. "Obviously we're not going back into the past to interfere – so what are we there for?" David tried to interrupt but she carried on. "It's tied up with the robbery – and the money."

"Maybe. Maybe we've got to do something with it. Like give it to the Animal Sanctuary?" David said suddenly.

Jenny stopped abruptly and he cannoned into her. "You've got it!" she said. "You've absolutely got it. I think—" She paused and then became more confident. "That's what Arthur would have wanted, isn't it? To stop the sanctuary closing. He would have wanted that more than anything."

"So we've got to come back and find the money," said David. "And fast."

"But suppose Ron took it? Suppose he murdered Arthur – *and* Bert!?"

"What did you see before you left?"

"Not a lot. Ron was still standing in front of Arthur with the knife. Bert was snarling—"

"And what did you do?"

"Grabbed at Ron's jacket. It wouldn't have stopped him, but I had to do something. I couldn't just stand there."

"I know," said David reassuringly. "But I've got an idea. Mum won't want to tell us about Arthur's murder – if he was murdered. She'd want to protect us. We've got to ask someone who's old enough to have been around at the time."

"What about the school caretaker? Len Large. He's been around forever."

"He's not exactly friendly, is he?"

"I get on with him all right," said Jenny confidently. "I think he's just lonely. He's got that big cat called Smudge – and if you're nice to Smudge—"

"We'll be nice to Smudge," said David. "Very nice indeed."

Brushing down their clothes, David and Jenny managed to get back into the school hall by the side door – and, more importantly, without being seen.

"Look at the clock," Jenny hissed. "We've only been away ten minutes. It's like time was suspended – and anyway, ten minutes was probably the time we took to get out of the shelter."

To be back in the present and amongst the familiar was so wonderful that the twins wanted to shout for joy, and for a few minutes they bathed in the wonderful, garish, noisy normality of it all. Unfortunately, this heady joy left them off guard.

Gary came up, looking arrogant. At first neither of the twins could make out what he was saying above the noise of the disco, but when they moved to the back of the hall Gary said more clearly, "Where you two been then?"

"Minding our own business," said David threateningly. "You been minding yours?"

"Why do you want to know?" asked Jenny woodenly.

"Just noticed you're both covered in cobwebs. Wondered why—"

Hours seemed to pass as they both stared at his grinning, foxy, freckled face. Neither of them could think of an answer.

"Cobwebs?" asked David, absent-mindedly brushing at his arm. "Cobwebs! How did they get there?" His mind was racing. He didn't dare look at Jenny, but he was sure she was as stumped as he was.

"Yes, cobwebs," said Gary, grinning even more widely. "Just what have you two been up to?"

"Up to?" David looked glassy-eyed, trying to turn it all into a joke. "What have we been up to?"

"Why do you keep repeating what I say?"

"Just winding you up," said Jenny calmly. "It's always good fun to see you gob-smacked. We had to go under the stage – get out some of the gear."

"I thought the disco came in from outside."

"Yeah." David followed his sister's lead. "It did. They just wanted some of those blocks to go behind one of the speakers. It's a bit wobbly." His explanation sounded lame but he delivered it with enough confidence to keep Gary guessing.

"Since when were you two allowed to help set up the disco?" he asked churlishly. He often felt left out of things and was always convinced there was a conspiracy to exclude him.

Jenny capitalised on this at once. "We were asked by Mr Decker," she said triumphantly. "Don't know why. Guess he likes us, that's all."

"Creep," said Gary, walking away.

"That was close." Jenny was sweating.

"Too close," replied David. "We'd better split up and—" The bitter cold swept back. The heat was gone in an instant.

"No," said Jenny. "Not yet. Not so soon. We're not ready—"

But nothing was changing and the dancers were still there, moving to the heavy beat.

"Look," said David. "Out in the playground."

Dimly, through the only open window, they could see a wraith-like Ron running, with Bert at his heels. Dodging the Labrador's snapping jaws, he disappeared towards the darkness of the road, obviously looking for a hiding place. Bert followed.

"Wasn't that blood on Ron's shirt?" asked Jenny. "I thought I saw a dark stain."

"Bert looked all right," said David.

"But what about Arthur? Do you think he's dead?"

CHAPTER EIGHT

Both Jenny and David found sleep difficult that night – their minds grappling endlessly with the events of the day before and what might yet be expected of them. Then there was their nagging concern for Arthur. But they still got up early, planning to see Len Large before school. After a rapid breakfast, during which their mother had predictably said, "I've never seen you two in such a hurry to get to school," they cycled off down the road, hoping that she was not too suspicious. As they neared the school another thought came into David's already overcrowded mind.

"What'll we do when we find the loot?"

"*If* we find it," Jenny hedged.

"Yeah. OK – if we find the loot. The police aren't going to let us give it to the Animal Sanctuary, are they? I mean it didn't belong to Arthur in the first place. He nicked it."

"There might be a reward," Jenny replied. "OK – the bank notes would be old, but they might be pleased to have them back. Barclays might give the Sanctuary some money."

David agreed that was possible. "I don't s'pose

Arthur's ghost has got much idea of time, has it?" he said.

"Bert certainly hasn't," replied Jenny.

Because they had a purpose, the twins felt buoyant, but always at the back of their minds was the certainty that the past would be reaching out again. Soon Bert would be back for them.

"What do you two want then?" Len Large wasn't exactly friendly, but then he never had been, particularly to David. He didn't like boys. They were a nuisance – and usually rude. But Jenny knew a bit about him – not much, but enough to reach him. His wife was dead and they had had no children. His dad was alive but he was in an old people's home up the road and Len lived in the school caretaker's bungalow – a drab building at the back of the playground. He only had Smudge for company and deeply missed his wife. To match his name, Len was a large, rather shambling sort of man with a spaniel-like face and sad, often suspicious eyes. He was particularly suspicious when he saw David, and Jenny wished she had come alone, but there was nothing she could do about that now. She just hoped that her brother would keep quiet – however unlikely that was. Unfortunately, he began the conversation.

"Can I see your Smudge?" he asked in a coy voice and Jenny winced.

"What for?"

"I like cats." David grinned from ear to ear and Jenny winced again. He looked as if he was pretending to be a cat now and she had a sudden memory-flash of the Cheshire Cat in *Alice in Wonderland*.

"You having me on?" Len's baggy face tightened.

"No," said David. "Jenny was telling me about Smudge."

"You seen him before."

"Not really."

"He's always out in the playground." Len was getting angrier by the second. "What's all this then? What you on about?"

"I think he's trying to say—" began Jenny.

"I know what I'm trying to say," snapped David who was tired and had a headache. "I want to see your cat."

"The point is," said Jenny. "We're thinking of getting one. Smudge has had loads of kittens, hasn't she? We just wondered if she was going to have any more."

At once Len calmed down. "I see. Matter of fact there's another litter due any day now," he said gruffly but more kindly, keeping his eyes on Jenny almost as if he were trying to blot out David's existence. "Would you be wanting one then?"

"If Mum agrees," said Jenny, knowing that she

wouldn't – and she would have to explain all that to Len later. Life was becoming more complicated by the moment. "But there's something else—"

"Yes?"

"About a relative of ours."

"Yes?" He was back to being hostile again – hostile and suspicious.

"Arthur. I need to find out about him for a school project."

"Who?"

"Arthur. Our mother's great uncle. I think his last name was Jackson. He was quite – quite a character round here and I thought you might have known him during the war. I mean – I know you would only have been a boy and—" Jenny stuttered to a halt for she could see a look of recognition in Len's eyes – but a look that was far from happy. Hurriedly, she prevented any denial. "So you did know him?"

"How do you make that out?" Len said warily.

"You had that look." Her voice was soft and gentle, and she was hoping against hope that David wouldn't decide to interfere. "That special re-membering look."

Len was startled. "Well – I don't know that I should tell you that much about Arthur Jackson."

"We know he was a villain," she said.

"He certainly was." Len permitted himself a slight chuckle, but the smile quickly disappeared from his face. "In fact he was a thief. Nick anything. He was a legend round our way. My older brother used to know him well."

"Didn't he rob banks?" asked David.

"I believe he did," said Len stiffly, speaking to him for the first time.

"Did your father know him?" asked Jenny.

"Not at all," he replied firmly.

"What we want to know is", continued David with crushing directness, "was he murdered?"

"Murdered?"

"Murdered by a man called Ron."

Jenny watched the shock sweeping over Len's crumpled features, and wondered why David's question had triggered such a strong reaction.

Len struggled to regain his composure. "No," he said with heavy conviction. "Arthur wasn't murdered."

"Are you sure?" asked Jenny.

"Absolutely. He died of a heart attack."

"When he was threatened with a knife?" David asked bluntly.

"Don't know." But once again the shock was in his eyes.

"The day of an air raid?" David persisted.

Len shook his head. "As far as I know he was found in the shelter alone. His dog was with him."

That doesn't tell us anything, thought David. "Did you know this Ron?" he asked.

"Ron? I don't know no Ron."

They had agreed to tell him nothing about the hidden money but David blurted it out just the same.

"Our mum says there's a rumour that he hid the proceeds of a bank raid in the shelter. And someone else told us this Ron tried to get it off him – or some of it. He was owed a share from another job."

David paused, and they watched more alarm roll across Len's features. Or were they just imagining it all?

"Dunno anything about that."

There was a long silence, interrupted by the school bell.

"So you can't help us any more?" Jenny pressed him desperately.

"No." There was a grim finality to his tone. "Tell you what though."

"What?" asked Jenny. "Have you remembered something else?"

"Not about Arthur. But it's funny you should mention that old shelter."

"Yes?" said David apprehensively.

"I've got this feeling kids are poking about in it."

"But it's out of bounds," said Jenny a little too quickly, and David added, "No one ever goes anywhere near it."

"I'm not so sure."

"What makes you think so?"

"That young Gary reckons he saw a couple of kids come out."

"Did he?" Jenny now knew she had to be very careful and daren't even shoot her brother a warning glance. "When was that?"

"He wouldn't say."

"That wasn't much help," David commented.

"I took a look this morning," replied Len slowly. "And I saw one of the doors was open. So I secured it. But that's not enough. I'm going to board it over when I get the wood." There was a long silence. Then he said, "That was the bell. Best be running along then."

"So we can have one of Smudge's kittens?" said Jenny, knowing she was sealing her own fate with Mum but anxious to leave on a less dramatic note. It would also open up the opportunity of cross-examining Len again.

He nodded and then smiled at her, the smile lighting up his whole face. It made him look quite different. "Course you can. Providing your parents agree."

"They will," said Jenny.

"There's something else," he said.

"Yes?"

"OK – Arthur Jackson was a bit of a Robin Hood, but don't run away with the idea that he was soft. Arthur was as hard as nails – and dangerous with it."

"I'll buy some new batteries for that torch and we'll go back in the shelter after school today," said David boldly. "I'm not going to wait for Bert to contact us again. If he wants to show us that's up to him, but we can make a search on our own. I want to get all this over with."

"What about Len? He said he'd fixed the door." Jenny knew David was right to take the initiative, but they had to be cautious.

"It'll be a bodge-up job, you'll see. He's famous for that."

Jenny looked at David doubtfully. He seemed too confident now. "What about Gary," she added, bringing up the next problem.

"I'll sort him out."

She almost lost her temper at his recklessness. "You can't! We must be careful or we'll draw attention to what we're doing." Then she hurried on to the plan she had devised. "It's Friday and there's nothing on after school. We'll have to hide somewhere."

"What about the storeroom in the gym? The lock's broken and it's always swinging open – just like the shelter."

"OK," said Jenny. "I'll ring Mum and say we've got a—"

"Detention?"

"Don't be daft. I know – a practice for sports day. We'll hide in the storeroom and then we'll have to dodge Len – and maybe even Gary."

"Gary would never wait after school," said David scornfully.

"No? He might. Think how nosy he is. Think how much he'd like to catch us out."

"OK." Her twin gave in. "I'll buy the batteries at lunch-time."

"Be careful," Jenny warned him again. "If anyone spots you and gets suspicious, we'll have had it – and so will Arthur and Bert, and the Sanctuary."

As she pushed open the door of the pupils' entrance to the school, Mr Decker was standing inside.

"Hello there. A little late this morning."

"Sorry, sir," they chorused uneasily.

"We can't have these discos if you get to bed so late that you miss your schooling," he began censoriously. "Of course, I realise we were forced into having it on a Thursday rather than our usual Friday. I have apologised to the parents, but the disco was in such demand, I did have to rely on the co-operation of all pupils." He bared his teeth at them in an imitation of a smile but his eyes were flinty cold.

"I'm sorry, sir," said Jenny. "Actually we got up very early and we were here at 8.30, but I wanted one of Mr Large's kittens and we got talking."

"I see. Well, perhaps next time you could do your talking after school, Jenny. Now, why are you both shivering? It's warm this morning. I hope you haven't got colds – we'll have them all round the school in a—"

At exactly that moment, Bert padded up and began to lick Jenny's wrist with his chilly tongue.

Jenny and David hurried into school, conscious that Bert was not following them as they thought he might but seemed to have taken off after Mr Decker. Maybe he was going to explore his office, thought David. Did Bert have some sixth sense about the Jaffa Cakes Mr Decker kept in there and was rumoured to consume by the packet each day, often nipping out for more at lunch time. Addiction to Jaffa Cakes had been Mr Decker's chief claim to fame for years.

"I know what you're up to," said Gary at break.

The suddenness of his attack almost caught David by surprise, but being more prepared now, his fast reactions came to the rescue. "Don't get you."

"You're going into the shelter," Gary continued in a childishly sing-song voice. "You didn't go under the stage at all, did you? Your clothes were covered in cobwebs because you went into the shelter. And do you know how I know?"

"What do you know?"

"I saw you coming out."

David looked hard into Gary's eyes. It was impossible to tell whether he was lying or not. "We've never been in that shelter in our lives," he replied quietly. "You know it's out of bounds." David slightly raised his voice. "I hope you're not thinking of going into the shelter, Gary. Mr Large is making it secure today. Apparently one of the doors has come open." He paused. "Is that anything to do with you, Gary?"

They were standing in the playground, and as David blurted it out a small crowd began to gather, hoping for a fight. The crowd rapidly grew.

"I saw you," said Gary, flummoxed by David's confident attitude.

"Rubbish."

"You're lying."

"Don't you call me a liar." To the gathering interest of the crowd, David moved nearer to Gary, prodding him in the chest. Then he gave him a push. "Don't you *ever* call me a liar."

"You're going to get it," muttered Gary.

"Get what?" David pushed him in the chest again, this time much harder, knowing he was running a big risk. Gary was tough and he had already had a couple of fights with him, both of which he had only marginally won. But even if he won another, they would both be in trouble.

"I'll get you!" threatened Gary, diving at him.

For a moment they locked arms until one of the crowd shouted, "Miss Timmen's coming!" In an instant everyone dispersed while the would-be combatants jumped apart, casually going their separate ways as if nothing had happened.

"What was all that?" hissed Jenny as she hurried past him.

"A warning, that's all," whispered David. "A warning to be even more careful than before."

The twins hid in the storeroom for an hour after school, giving all the pupils and teachers enough time to leave the buildings. As the time trickled slowly past David and Jenny grew increasingly tense, but they knew that to come out too early could be disastrous. Eventually, Jenny said, "Let's give it a swing."

"OK. I've got the new batteries and the torch is really powerful now."

"It had better be," she said sternly. "We can't afford any mistakes."

"We're not going to make any," replied David.

They crept out of the entrance to the gym which was opposite the shelter, but the playground was a vast desert stretching in front of them, and when the twins looked up at the buildings they imagined dozens of eyes watching them. Particularly Gary's. And where was Len Large? They waited a couple of minutes crouched in the doorway, each unable to give the signal to go ahead – their minds buzzing with instruction and counter-instruction.

Finally, David said, "Let's go."

The twins walked swiftly across the playground, the school looming over them as if the buildings were on the move, closing in on them. David was certain that the Assembly Hall was nearer, the boiler room was encroaching, the old and new classroom blocks towering over them, the bike sheds edging closer. Shadows, shadows with eyes, seemed to move at every window. A gentle gust of wind swept an ice-cream wrapper towards them. It seemed to make an incredible rattling sound on the hard tarmac as the gentle wind suddenly became an icy blast.

Bert appeared from nowhere, wagging his tail and barking. Although the twins could still see through him and knew that no one else could see him at all, the ghostly noise rang in their ears and they abandoned their fast walk and broke into a pell-mell run.

Bert overtook him, and as Jenny and David reached the air raid shelter, they stood and looked back fearfully. Nothing moved; even the icy wind had dropped. David had never seen the school buildings so lifeless. Now, rather than looming over him, they were like cardboard cut-outs or the fort he had had as a little boy. He just couldn't believe they were real any more.

"Come on!" Jenny hissed. "Someone will see us."

They had run the last few yards with Bert bounding happily beside them. Then he trotted down to the shelter door and disappeared straight through it, his tail still wagging.

Jenny made an inspection. "You're right," she said. "It's a Len Large bodge-up. He's just tied it with cord." She began to unpick the knot. "This isn't going to take long." It didn't. Jenny had the door open again a few seconds later, only to find Bert panting on the threshold. "It's all very well for you," she said.

David carefully closed the rusty door of the shelter, but there was no way he could re-attach the cord and if Len Large came out to check, it would be all too obvious that someone had gone in. He could only rely on the caretaker's natural laziness.

At once, the dark closed in on them and the fear returned, suffusing them with panic. Could they really go through this again, the twins wondered miserably; the smell, the unknown dangers, the unpredictable Bert who might be friend or foe, the sinister Arthur and murderous Ron, all awaited them in the tunnel. But the strong beam of the torch made the journey easier this time as the twins picked their way through the discarded wreckage of so many decades. Bert bounded ahead, waiting every few yards rather as if he was rounding them up; David had never seen him so purposeful.

Once they had arrived at the end of the tunnel, Jenny said, "We won't bother searching here – we'll start behind the sandbags." Immediately Bert was beside them, and now his cold nuzzling was not only urgent but aggressive too. It was as though the Labrador knew that time was running out for him.

CHAPTER NINE

Amazingly, the Command Post was virtually intact, although covered in dust and much decayed. The chairs were missing but the long table remained, covered in boxes. The filing cabinet was still there, but the side table had disappeared. The picture of the King was at a crazy angle on the wall, its glass dark with damp and mildew, but the royal face could just be seen.

"Bert's messing about with one of those sandbags," said David. "Let's take a look."

They both crouched down and he shone the torch. Several bags were empty and they wondered if the sand had been removed deliberately, but there was nothing inside and the remainder were damply full. Meanwhile, Bert was sitting beside them, watching intently, as if testing out their intelligence and persistence.

"Nothing here," said David, but Bert responded with a long, loud growl as if this negative comment was not nearly good enough.

Jenny continued to scrabble away. "Go and look in the filing cabinet," she commanded. "I'll carry on. We need to be absolutely sure."

"Arthur wouldn't hide the money in a filing cabinet," said David crossly. "Not unless he was crazy." Nevertheless, he pulled open the drawers, only to discover them empty of anything but mould.

Glancing around him, David felt deeply disappointed. He had been so sure of finding the money, of—

"Look at this!" To his amazement, Jenny was holding up a bank note. There was no doubt about it. A fifty pound note bearing the King's head.

Both the twins were trembling with excitement as David returned to the sandbags.

"Where did you find it?"

"Stuck to the inside of this empty bag, which means other notes must have been there – once."

"Ron?"

"Maybe, or Arthur—"

"What do you mean?"

"Well, he might have shifted them, made a new hiding place—"

David wasn't so sure. "You know what – someone could have found them any time since the war. It's all over, Jenny. The money's gone."

"What's that?" whispered Jenny.

"A light," hissed David. "Get down. It must be Len."

"Now we're in trouble," she said apprehensively. Behind them, Bert stiffened and the familiar blast of stale, cold air surrounded the twins.

The figure kept on coming through the darkness. David had snapped off his torch immediately but he was sure it must have been seen. He looked desperately at Bert, but he was becoming fainter every moment.

The oncoming figure paused at the kitchen area, flashing a beam over the debris. The twins crouched down even lower behind the sandbags but they could hear slow, hesitant footsteps approaching. We've had it, Jenny thought as the light probed just above her head. The twins hunched themselves up against its threat until they saw a dark shape a few centimetres away and the strong beam swept over them.

Jenny saw the all too familiar face first, the freckles like a livid rash on the white skin and the frightened, staring eyes. It wasn't Len. It was Gary.

David was on his feet before Jenny could scramble to hers, but already the reality about them was dissolving and the air around them was even colder. Gary melted away as the air raid siren howled and they heard the sound of Bert barking in the distance.

"Children," said Miss Perry. "Children – listen to me. We're going to sit here for a while. Leonard!" she shouted. "Leonard Large. Stop talking at once and sit down with the others. I don't want to have to speak to you again."

The low watt bulbs glowed, and in the dim light Jenny and David could see Miss Perry's pupils sitting on benches and gazing up at her. All except a rather large, fat boy with a puffy face. There was no doubt in the twins' minds that this was Len Large as a schoolboy. He hadn't changed much.

Once more, Miss Perry's pupils had their gas masks in front of them and the siren was howling, beginning to drown Bert's barking.

Now, the dimly lit tunnels were filling up with people, this time mackintoshed and overcoated. Clearly the season had changed and there was a smell of wet clothes. It must be raining outside, thought Jenny, wondering how many months had passed. Or could it be that time had moved back?

The siren faded; there was a long silence and then an explosion – very close. All the lights in the shelter went out and they were plunged into darkness.

"Do you think they'll hit the school, miss?" asked Len.

"I'm sure they won't," she replied.

"Why not, miss?"

"Be quiet, Leonard." Her voice was reassuringly authoritative.

From one of the tunnels came the sound of prayers.

"Arthur might be dead," whispered Jenny. "I can't see him anywhere."

"We don't know where we are in time," hissed David.

More dust rained down and some of the children were sobbing. Miss Perry began to sing:

> *Oh God, our help in ages past,*
> *Our hope for years to come,*
> *Our shelter from the stormy blast,*
> *And our eternal home.*

Her voice was strong and clear and the hymn was taken up by some of the other adults as well as the children, and David and Jenny felt more confidence radiating round the shelter. Towards the end of the first verse the lights came on again and the twins were able to search the shadows for Arthur. Was he dead or alive? They didn't know which was the more frightening thought.

Then, to their amazement, Arthur, looking fit and well, briskly emerged from the kitchen pushing his trolley. "Now who's for a treat?" He grinned at Miss Perry's pupils and David and Jenny could see that he was no longer hostile and brooding but generous and happy. There was no doubt that there were two very distinct sides to this strange and contradictory man. 'I've got a couple of boxes of biscuits. With a bit of luck, there should be one each."

"We can't afford them," said Miss Perry sharply.

"No matter. They're all free."

"Free?"

"Yeah. Fell off the back of a lorry," he confided to her in a stage whisper. "Now, who's for one of these?" Dozens of eager hands shot up.

"Really!" Miss Perry frowned and then suddenly relented with her kind, tolerant smile. "The milk monitors will hand them out. And keep that dog of yours under control, Arthur," she added severely as Bert jumped up at the biscuit tin.

"So," said Jenny. "Arthur's still alive."

"If we're forward in time." David was still cautious. He had a very unsettled feeling as he watched the events of over fifty years ago unfold. It was a ghost world now – the adults would be long dead – but David wondered if he might know any of the children, like Len, as old people in Hockley. What an extraordinary conversation they would have if he told them all about what he had seen in the shelter. But that would be interfering with time, and the twins were at its mercy. He shuddered at the thought.

"I'm sure we are," Jenny said optimistically.

"Then Ron's still around somewhere," he warned. David pondered for a while. "And if he's still alive, he probably knows about the money too."

"So he could have taken it?" asked Jenny.

"Could have, and there's another thing," said David. "Do you think that time really is kind?"

"What on earth do you mean?" Jenny stared at her twin, mystified.

"It's hiding us. Don't you realise it took us away directly Gary showed up."

"Just a coincidence."

"I'm not so sure." David turned back to Miss Perry's children, all of whom were now eating biscuits with Arthur looking on, his face wreathed in a kindly smile.

"Wish I'd had kids, Miss P," he said. "Never got round to it somehow."

"You're a busy man," she replied and Jenny wondered if there was a trace of sarcasm in her voice. Did she know he was a crook?

"That's true."

"I hear the shop's sold — and the van."

"All for a profit," Arthur replied with satis-faction.

Well, thought David. That certainly puts us in the right time. He looked at Jenny and she nodded.

Miss Perry turned back to her pupils. "And now we're going to sing our hearts out, aren't we, children? We're going to sing, *Run, Rabbit, Run*." She burst into song.

Run, rabbit,
Run, rabbit,
Run, run, run.
Here comes the farmer with his gun, gun, gun.
He'll get by, without his rabbit pie,
So run, rabbit,
Run, rabbit,
Run, run, run.

As the children's singing continued, it was taken up by everyone else in the tunnels. Gradually the song grew louder and more rhythmic – and more unified. Arthur started to push his tea trolley round, singing in a rich baritone, winking at Miss Perry as he passed. Miss Perry winked back.

When David turned to Jenny he saw that her eyes were full of tears. "What's up?"

"They're all so happy and brave," she said. "I don't want them to die."

"They won't all be dead even now," he replied. "But I don't want them to change – to grow up. Is that unfair?"

Jenny shook her head. "I know what you mean," she said.

The singing changed to *The White Cliffs of Dover*, and as it swelled, Bert bounded across their vision. A light cold mist rose from the floor and the ghosts of Miss Perry and the children began to fade away.

When the mist parted they were still in the shelter, but no one else was there.

"It's as if Bert changed the scene," said David.

They waited, listening to the sound of footsteps coming from the entrance tunnel. Who could it be? Arthur? Ron? Len? Gary? The steps continued, solid and determined, and there was also a scampering sound. Bert must be there too.

This time the cold was so intense that the twins could hardly bear it, but there was also a loud ticking sound. They looked round for a clock but there wasn't one. Then Jenny remembered the loud tick of the clock in the ghostly school hall which had appeared in the middle of the disco. Was time warning them that it was beginning to run out?

Then Arthur arrived. His mackintosh was wringing wet and he was no longer his kind self; instead he seemed threatening but ill. He was followed by Bert, looking forlorn and bedraggled.

Arthur held a large canvas grip which had a zip down one side. He looked worried and had obviously been running, his breath coming in little gasps and his face the colour of a suet pudding.

He went straight into the Command Post and the twins followed, Bert at their heels now, as if he were rounding them up like sheep. The back wall was a mixture of hard-packed earth and rock, partly supported by sandbags and partly by props.

Arthur stood there for a while listening, making absolutely certain that no one was coming through the tunnel, and when Bert began to whine he abruptly told him to be quiet. Once he had assured himself that there was no sound of pursuit, Arthur reached up to a large stone embedded in the packed earth and began to pull. Slowly and with a great effort he managed to prise it loose. Then he began on another and another and another until he had made a large gap into which he thrust his arm.

Darting a glance behind him, he listened, started, and then hurriedly began to replace the stones. He worked at the most incredible speed, but it was obvious that the effort was getting to him – as well as the anxiety of wondering who was coming down the tunnel.

Jenny and David strained their ears to listen for approaching footsteps, but the noise Arthur was making was too loud for the twins to hear anything else. He was wheezing and gasping in the most alarming way and the colour in his face had changed from the suety hue to a nasty mauve. He managed to replace the last stone, however, and turned away from the back wall, trying to rub the dirt off his hands. Seeing a half full washing up bowl he plunged them in, desperately rubbing one hand against the other and then drying them with a towel.

Arthur's gasping and wheezing didn't stop, even when he stood listening again, but he managed to walk slowly from the Command Post to the large area in front with its tables and chairs. Bert followed, agitated and restless, and the twins brought up the rear.

Arthur propped himself up on the wall, his face twisting in pain, still listening intently. Meanwhile, Bert was growling, his hackles rising. He had a wary look in his big, moist eyes.

The sound along the tunnel was no more than a tiny movement, but it came as the final blow to Arthur. With a strangled cry he clasped his chest, bent over and staggered. For a moment and with tremendous effort he drew himself up, and then pitched forward on to the floor with a groan. He lay face down without moving and the twins stared at him in horrified disbelief.

Bert padded over to Arthur, whining and licking the back of his neck, but there was not the slightest sign of life.

Was he dead? The twins knelt down beside him, David trying to take his wrist and seeing his hand go right through it – and Jenny finding the same with Arthur's brawny neck.

All they could feel was a more intense cold as Bert licked their hands, silently pleading with them to do something – anything – to save his master. The ticking of time's clock increased to a frenzy – and then stopped completely. The silence spread until it seemed equally deafening.

CHAPTER TEN

The sound from the tunnel came again and again. Jenny and David realised that slowly and cautiously someone was moving towards them.

Bert stood by Arthur, still licking his neck, but his hackles began to rise again as Miss Perry appeared, looking afraid.

Directly she saw Bert snarl and heard the deep, vicious growling, she came to an abrupt and uneasy halt. "Arthur," she said softly, and then more loudly, "Arthur? I saw you run down here and you didn't look well. A police car drove past—"

Bert growled even more ferociously.

"You all right, Arthur?" Miss Perry moved a little nearer. "Arthur?"

There was no reply, and as she advanced she saw him lying on the floor. Hurriedly, Miss Perry walked over to him. Ignoring Bert's protective growls, she knelt down beside Arthur, loosened his collar and gasped out something they couldn't hear. Then Miss Perry rose shakily to her feet and muttered, "I'll get help. I'll get help now."

She ran back towards the tunnel and Bert began to bark furiously.

"We've got to get to him," said Jenny.

"You know we can't," said David. "Arthur's been dead for years. This is when he died – that's all."

"We can't just leave him there."

"Of course we can. Miss Perry will be back soon with some help."

Bert padded over to Arthur and resumed licking his face, pausing now and then to whine in distress. Then, suddenly, the Labrador left his master and came over to them, wagging his tail, clearly pleading with David and Jenny to intervene.

"There's nothing we can do," said Jenny, the tears pouring down her cheeks.

"We're not in the right time," added David, knowing Bert would never understand, then or now.

But the Labrador wasn't going to give in easily and he jumped up at him, his paws once again lightly resting on his shoulders. He rocked David to and fro and then began to work on Jenny.

Suddenly, a great hissing sound filled their ears, as if air was running out of a bicycle tyre. The shelter grew dim and blackness enclosed them, the hissing sound becoming even louder.

"What's the matter with you two?" asked Gary.
"You seen a ghost?" His freckled face was as white
and staring and frightened as when they had left
him seemingly hours ago. But, David realised
quickly, they probably hadn't left him at all.

"What are you doing here?" Jenny sounded
officious. "You aren't allowed in this old shelter."

"Neither are you," said Gary, waving his torch
in their faces.

"You watch yourself," replied David but Jenny
laid a restraining hand on his arm.

"Now let's get one thing straight." David
sounded confident. "We've got a very special
reason to be down here, and I'm going to have to
swear you to absolute secrecy – if you want to get
anything out of it that is."

"What do you mean – anything out of it?" Gary
was suspicious but he was also interested.

"A few days ago we saw the caretaker – Len
Large – come out of here, looking – sort of
disappointed."

"Disappointed?" echoed Gary. But he was
clearly hooked.

"Don't interrupt!" said David crisply, while
Jenny looked at him in horror. What was he
doing, implicating innocent Len like this? Or was
he saying the first thing that came into his head –

as usual? "We followed him and looked through the window of his house. He had a thin bundle of notes – money – and he was counting them. Anyway, we've explored the shelter a couple of times and found a load more. The bank will pay a big reward for this and we'll give you a share if you don't tell."

Gary studied their faces in his foxy way. "How can I believe you?" he asked.

"Here's the evidence." David twitched the dusty old fifty pound note with the King's head on it from Jenny, and Gary's eyes seemed to bulge from his head like a frog that had seen a particularly succulent fly.

"Wow! Is that real?"

"Of course it's real, but it's old – and we've got to find the rest of the loot before Len does."

"How will he know where to look?" asked Gary suspiciously.

Jenny could see that he wasn't swallowing David's story and didn't know whether to be glad or sorry.

"He came here as a kid in the war. Maybe he noticed something."

This was the weakest part of her twin's dubious explanation, thought Jenny, and Gary didn't look as if he was entirely convinced.

"This reward," said Gary greedily. "Will it be much?"

"Yes, it should be, but if you grass us up then you'll get nothing."

"How do you know where to look?"

"We think we know exactly where it is," said David.

"Where?"

"We can't tell you that," said Jenny abruptly.

"Why not?"

"How could we trust *you*?"

Gary was silent. He could see the sense of that, but the situation seemed to be deadlocked. Then he decided to give them a chance. "How long do you want?" he asked grudgingly.

"Another day."

"Why can't you search now?"

"Because of Len. He told us he was going to check the shelter tonight – he'd seen the cord had been tampered with."

"By you?"

"Yes. We don't want to run the risk of getting caught, so we're stepping up the search to-morrow," Jenny answered, deciding to give her brother some support.

"Can't I come?"

"No way," muttered David.

"Why not?" Gary was aggressive again.

"Because three's a crowd," said Jenny quickly. "But if you don't tell on us, we'll give you a third of the reward, won't we, Dave?"

"Suppose we'll have to." He knew his unwilling agreement would sound more authentic.

"All right then," said Gary. He was thinking fast now and they both knew they couldn't trust him at all.

Then David had an idea. "Dirty down here, isn't it?"

"What do you mean?"

"Well – you saw cobwebs on our clothes last night."

"Yeah."

"You've been careful, haven't you?" he persisted. "Very careful. So you could come out of the shelter nice and clean and then grass us up. Say you hadn't been in but you saw us coming out. That kind of grassing."

"I wouldn't do that," protested Gary. "You said you'd give me a cut. I believe you." But the cunning look in his eyes convinced the twins that he only half believed them and was hedging his bets. There was no telling what he would do and David knew they would have to take precautions.

"I don't trust you."

"No?"

"But you'll be a lot more trustworthy if you're not so clean." With that, David suddenly grabbed Gary in a rugby tackle and they fell to the ground. The fight was brief and to the point. David had the advantage of surprise and was soon on top.

"You're not exactly Mr Clean now," he panted as he put his knees on Gary's shoulders. "So it's going to be a bit tricky for you to secretly grass us up to Len. He won't let anyone get away with being in this shelter."

"Let me up!" yelled Gary.

"I wouldn't make too much noise if I were you."

"Just let me up," he yelled again and David rose to his feet.

"I'll get you for this!"

"Not if you want the reward you won't," Jenny warned him.

Gary was up now, trembling with rage and advancing on David. But he paused. "You'd better be right," he said as if he had very reluctantly decided to give them the benefit of the doubt.

"Oi – what's going on!" came a familiar voice.

Although they couldn't see him, there was no doubt that Len Large was hurrying down the tunnel with a torch that was casting a dazzlingly sharp beam.

"Go for the exit," whispered Jenny. "Now."

The three of them raced up the other branch of tunnel as silently as they could, not daring to 	on their torches and blundering into every 	bject. David hoped against hope that they 	the outside before Len realised where 	he was quick enough, the caretaker could easily pick them out with the beam of his torch.

Jenny had never run so fast in her life. She was in front of the two boys and some sixth sense enabled her to avoid cannoning into most of the debris.

"Shut up," panted David as Gary squealed with fear. "As soon as we're out of here, you get clear of the school – fast. OK?"

"OK," he gasped, struggling to keep up as Jenny ran even faster, but with a thump and groan he fell over an old bicycle.

"Get up!"

"I can't."

"You've got to," Jenny insisted. "You've got to get up!" Any moment she was sure she would see Len pounding down the tunnel towards them, his strong beam identifying each one of them. What would happen when Mr Decker found out? It just didn't bear thinking about.

"My foot's caught."

Both Jenny and David searched for Gary's leg in the darkness, but only managed to pull off one of his trainers.

"It's the other one," he hissed.

"What?"

"The other one." He gave a little whinny of pain.

Jenny searched again, found his foot and

wrenched it free of the rusty old bike. "Get up!"

Gary rose shakily to his feet.

"It's not far now," whispered Jenny. "You can see the light. Go for it!"

He hobbled on, speeding up as she aimed a kick at him.

"Len's torch will pick us out any minute," hissed David.

Gary's hobble became a run.

At last the three of them emerged from the tunnel, cautiously opened the door, gazed around the deserted playground and then raced for the school gate. They were filthy, dishevelled and desperately out of breath. What was more, passers-by on the street were staring at them. Then David saw Mrs Craddock.

"It's her," he gasped. "The biggest mouth in East London."

"We can't avoid her," Jenny panted, but Gary could as he streaked off towards home.

Mrs Craddock gave them a confiding smile, her long narrow face riddled with curiosity. "Well – Jenny and David. Where are you going in such a hurry?"

"Home," gasped Jenny flatly, unable for the moment to be more inventive.

Fortunately, David had an inspiration. "We've been on a run," he said.

"I can see that." She smiled sweetly.

"A cross-country run, I mean."

"Don't you wear sports kit for that?" Her false teeth came together in a sharp, disapproving click.

"We forgot it."

"Forgot it, dear?"

"Yeah – so they made us run in our school clothes."

"What a pity."

"Yes," said Jenny, joining in at last. "Mum will be furious."

"She should be cross with the school, not you," said Mrs Craddock with sudden and surprising sympathy. Then Jenny remembered how she hated Mr Decker who had suspended her son last year – a wimp of a boy called Alan who kept stealing from other pupils. It was one of the few good things Mr Decker had done. "It's outrageous, making you run in your good school clothes. Absolutely outrageous."

"Better be going now," said David, afraid that Len Large might appear at any moment. "We both need a wash."

"I should think you do," agreed Mrs Craddock with what she meant to be a kind smile but came across as a patronising smirk.

The miracle was that their mother was out visiting a friend after work and the house was empty. The twins washed their hands and faces quickly, then concentrated on getting the dust and dirt off their clothes. David's were covered in debris after his self-sacrificing fight with Gary. Somehow they managed to get most of the mess off his trousers which had taken the worst battering.

"It's going to be even more difficult to get into the playground on a Saturday," said Jenny. "We'll have to be there really early – and by the way, I think it was rotten of you to drop Len into it all. He's not a crook."

"At dawn?" asked David as they sat down to cans of coke and a well-earned stack of toast. Their father wouldn't be in for another hour so they were free to make plans. "And as for Len – I'm not so sure. He could've remembered something he'd overheard about Arthur and the money. Done his own search."

"Only he didn't," said Jenny and David quickly changed the subject in case it became an argument.

"Mum and Dad lie-in on a Saturday. Can't we say we're meeting some friends to go – to go skating? The rink opens at eight."

"All right." Jenny bit into her fourth slice of toast. She had never felt so hungry and David obviously felt the same.

"Len could well have been searching that shelter for years," insisted David. He felt better now that he'd eaten and was prepared to push his theory about Len a bit further. "I'm sure he knows about the money but just can't find it."

"How do we find out?" asked Jenny sceptically.

"Chat him up."

"You mean, just walk up and say: By the way, have you found any money in that shelter yet? Or are you still looking?" Jenny scoffed. "Maybe Ron found the money. There's no real way of telling if it's still there and we've got no evidence that Len's been searching. Either way, I bet you we're too late."

David frowned, unwilling to accept her pessimism. "Bert wouldn't have contacted us if the money had been found. It's all too much of a coincidence – the Animal Sanctuary going bust and Bert showing up in the school. It's the one cause Arthur was devoted to – more than anything else."

Jenny nodded, taking a long drink of the coke that was now warm from standing on the table so long. David had almost managed to convince her at last. "And Gary? We're taking a big risk with him," he said.

"I think he'll keep his mouth shut, as long as he thinks there's something in it for him," said David, but he sounded doubtful. "After all – what can he do? What can he prove now?"

"He doesn't trust us," replied Jenny. She was

exhausted but wanted to be sure they'd thought of everything.

"And we don't trust him and never will," said David. "So what's new?"

"Suppose he sets up an ambush for us to-morrow?" she persisted.

"We can soon suss that out tomorrow morning. Don't forget we've got Bert on our side."

"He's not always a lot of use in an emergency, is he?" said Jenny. "And why should he be? He's only a dog – and a ghost dog at that."

"Maybe." David suddenly sounded more confident."But don't forget we saw Arthur die. Bert's on his own now."

CHAPTER ELEVEN

David took a long time getting off to sleep that night, and when he did he dreamt of Bert.

The Labrador was in his bedroom, and standing beside him was Arthur, looking rather better than when he had last seen him. Instead of being cold, David was warm, and rather than appearing sinister and hostile, Arthur was jaunty and friendly. He looked very flash, wearing a dark suit David hadn't seen before and had a carnation in his buttonhole. He was freshly shaved and his hair oiled down with Brylcreem. "You know where it is," Arthur said to David. "Go and get it. We've got to save the Sanctuary and you're the boy to do it."

He then gave David a stiff little bow and began to side-step out of his bedroom, singing, "I'll trust you if you'll trust me, and we'll meet again by the old oak tree." The rhythm was catchy and David soon found himself singing along with him while Bert sat there on his haunches, waving two paws in the air.

Then Arthur stopped singing and said, "You know where the old oak tree is, Dave, don't you?"

"It's in the road just outside the playground," he heard himself replying.

"Been there for years – before my time, and before yours." Arthur did an odd little shuffling dance out of the room, followed by Bert. Then he stuck his head round the bedroom door and said, "Don't try and double-cross me, will you?" The warmth suddenly changed to a freezing blast of cold air.

David woke, the words ringing in his ears, and looking at his watch saw that it was 7.30. He jumped out of bed, pulled on his clothes and hurried down to the kitchen where he found Jenny making toast and humming a little tune that had a familiar rhythm. The words danced in David's mind.

> *I'll trust you if you'll trust me,*
> *And we'll meet again by the old oak tree.*

"So you had the same dream as me?"

Jenny looked up and grinned. "He was in my room with Bert – and I wasn't cold."

"He was in mine too."

"He looked well and quite smart with that carnation in his buttonhole. Then he said, 'You know where it is. Go and get it. We've got to save the Animal Sanctuary and you're the girl to do it.'"

"Too right."

"But later on, he stuck his head round the bedroom door and it got so cold that—"

"I know the rest," said David hurriedly, before she could continue.

"There are two Arthur's, aren't there?" said Jenny. "And we've got to watch out for the one that's really evil."

As they walked cautiously past the school gates, David could see that the odds had already begun stacking against them.

"Do you see what I see?" he whispered.

Len Large and Gary were locked in conversation in the school playground.

"Quiet," hissed Jenny. "Back off!"

They took shelter behind the old oak tree that Arthur had sung about in their dream, and, at least partially concealed behind its enormous trunk, they watched and listened.

"I tell you," said Gary. "They're looking for the money that you've been searching for."

"Wish I'd never told you," grumbled Len. "Gave me a shock like – you asking me about that old money – or I wouldn't ever have confided in a stupid kid like you."

"Thanks a lot."

"The main point is they shouldn't have been down there. But I can't prove anything because I haven't caught 'em. Yet. But I'm going to keep an eye out—"

"Suppose they know where the money is?" asked Gary slowly.

"How could they?"

"Arthur was their mother's great uncle. Maybe it's been passed down the family like and—"

"Don't be daft. It would have been found years ago if that was the case."

"Suppose they just found out?" Gary was really pushing it now.

"How?"

"Maybe there was a message in an old trunk – or somewhere," he finished lamely.

Len laughed derisively. "It'll be a message in a bottle next."

"All I'm saying is that there'll be a reward, won't there?"

"Might be."

"And they'll get it – and give the money to the Sanctuary – just like Arthur wanted."

"How do you know all this?" demanded Len.

"My granddad told me. And when I saw them twins coming out of that shelter I put two and two together."

"And made five." But Len was clearly more interested now.

"Do you want to have a go at this or not? Or don't you need the money?" asked Gary cheekily.

"Now wait a minute—"

"We could share the reward. All we need is to watch those twins, grab 'em when they find the loot and—"

"Bob's your uncle," said Len.

"You mean you're on?"

"I'm certainly not going to allow kids trespassing in that shelter," said Len Large. "It's more than my job's worth."

"So what are we going to do?" asked Gary eagerly.

"Go home – and if anything happens I'll ring you there."

"You will?" Gary was suspicious.

"Trust me," said Len.

But Gary looked at him as if he definitely couldn't do any such thing.

When Gary had gone, Len walked slowly towards the entrance of the shelter. After fiddling with the cord, he opened the door and went inside.

"Now what?" said Jenny.

"Looks like we're in trouble," replied David dismally. "We can't go in now because Len's there, and if and when he comes out Gary might turn up. We've had it. I bet you he's hiding out somewhere. I bet he doesn't trust Len."

Jenny suddenly shivered. "Gone cold, hasn't it?" she said to her twin and saw that he was trembling.

The blast of urgent, icy air caught at their throats, making it even harder to breathe than it had before.

"I think Bert's on his way," David gasped.

Just then the Labrador loped around the corner and a wave of panic filled Jenny's mind. They could be arrested for what they were doing, but that was not her main worry. Suppose the ghostly presence of Arthur turned against them? Suppose he thought they were out to take the money for themselves? He was so unpredictable. One moment he could turn up in a dream, so warm and encouraging. The next he might turn murderously angry, especially if he thought they might double-cross him. And they didn't have a clue as to which Arthur might be around.

"Bert." Jenny knelt down beside him. "Can't you help us?"

"He already has," said David suddenly. "I've got this amazing idea. I'm going to ring the school bell. I've seen Len do it and it's just inside his office. That should flush him out."

"Not for long," said Jenny gloomily. "He'll just switch it off and go back to the shelter."

"Hang on. I remember Len used to lock his office door and pull the blinds down when he wanted a kip. Let's go and see if the door will lock from the outside."

"You mean—"

"Come on!" said David impatiently. "We haven't got time to talk."

Reluctantly, Jenny followed her twin. As usual, he didn't seem to be thinking about the consequences and she knew how serious they could be.

Bert sat down on his haunches, giving her a hostile look. Had he picked up her fear? Did he think they were going to let him down?

CHAPTER TWELVE

The twins ran across the playground, through the
school entrance and then down the corridor to
Len's office. It was a small, dark, windowless, little
cubbyhole just opposite the assembly hall and
contained a desk, a chair, a basket for Smudge,
filing cabinets, a cupboard stuffed full of brooms,
mops and cleaning materials – and the rather old-
fashioned apparatus that rang the bell.

"You sure you know how it works?" questioned
Jenny doubtfully.

"Yes," he replied confidently. "But how are we
going to lock him in?"

"What a minute. Let's unplug the telephone
first." With renewed determination, Jenny walked
into the little office that smelt of polish and stale
tea and ruthlessly pulled the phone lead out and
tucked the phone under some paper in the waste
bin. As she did so, she realised how frightened she
was becoming of Bert as well as Arthur. The
Labrador was getting desperate and she could feel
him driving her on now – almost as if he was
inside her. "If we hide behind the assembly hall

door – with a bit of luck he won't see who locked him in," Jenny gasped.

"Let's just check the key first."

"OK." Jenny took it out of the inside lock, fitted it into the outside and did a test. "It's fine, but the best thing to do is to take the key with us. Then he won't see it on the outside of the door."

"Suppose it won't go in?"

"I've shown you," she said impatiently. "It fits perfectly."

"I know," said David. "But we're going to be nervous. Our hands will be shaking."

"It's not a question of 'we'." Jenny was much more resourceful now. "Only one of us can do it – and they've got to be quick or he'll be out after us. So no fumbling."

David nodded. "What are we going to do? Toss up?"

"OK."

He felt in his pocket and drew out a coin. "Tails you do it – heads I do."

David tossed and then trapped the spinning coin under his foot. Nervously, he drew his shoe slowly away.

"It's heads," said Jenny.

David gulped.

"Ready?"

Jenny's hand was on the lever. "I'm ready."

"Let's go."

The bell rang with a terrible clamour.

"Behind the assembly hall door. Now," hissed David although there was no need for him to whisper as the noise was far too loud for anyone to hear them speak.

Making sure they couldn't possibly be seen from the corridor, the twins crouched down.

They waited such a long time that they were beginning to wonder whether Len was coming out of the shelter at all. Either he couldn't hear the violent ringing – or he had chosen to ignore it.

David glanced at his watch. Five minutes had passed but it seemed more like five hours. Then they heard the sound of running footsteps.

"Now," said Jenny as there was a slamming sound. She breathed a sigh of relief for she had been imagining how difficult it would be if he had left the office door open. David would have had to close it quietly – or as quietly as he could – fit the key in the lock and turn it. At any time during that process, Len could have whipped round and seen him.

David crept out into the corridor, taking care not to reach the level of the glass pane in the door of the office. Then, with a hand that was shaking so much he could hardly grip the key, he inserted it in the lock just as the bell stopped ringing. He turned the key as quietly as he could, tested the handle and then ran back to Jenny, signalling her to get moving. Fast.

As they tore down the corridor, the twins heard Len's roar of rage when he tried to open the door. Then he yelled, "Who's playing funny games, eh? Who's playing games?"

David and Jenny paused, checked for Gary and then ran across the playground, heading for the air raid shelter. They could only hear him yelling dimly now and they were thankful for the thick brick walls of the Victorian building. Unless anyone came close they wouldn't hear him, and maybe he would be so hoarse by then that he would have stopped shouting.

Even so, they both knew that they wouldn't have much time in the shelter. Could they find the money before Len managed to get out – or Gary turned up again?

"I left the key in the lock," gasped David.

"Never mind."

"I should have brought it with me."

"It doesn't matter." Jenny was reassuring. "Get your torch out."

The door to the shelter was half open and they could just see Bert's nose snuffling inside. There was no doubt he was waiting for them and an icy blast urged them on.

★

David swept the beam in a wide-ranging arc as they ran down the tunnel, with the Labrador following, panting and giving little yelps of excitement.

Finally, they arrived at the Command Post.

"He stood here," said David. "He pulled out some stones and there was an inner wall of packed earth. That's where the money was."

"It was loose then," warned Jenny. "But I should think all the damp has made it rigid now."

"Or looser." He began to pull at the wall but nothing gave, and although he got a grip on some of the larger stones, they refused to budge.

"I'm sure it was here," said David in rising frustration, conscious all the time that Len might be hurrying vengefully towards them. "Where else could it have been?"

"Try a bit higher up. He was taller than you."

David reached up as far as he could and with considerable effort pulled at a jagged stone. It moved, sending a cloud of dust into his eyes. Choking, he fell back.

"Get the table," said Jenny urgently. "And push it further over. Then we can both stand on it." She picked up a broken chair leg. "I'll use this to get a bit of leverage."

Hurriedly, both desperately conscious of time running out on them, the twins pushed the table hard against the wall and stood on it, pulling and probing, levering and scrabbling at the surface. At last, first one stone came out and then another and another, sending up clouds of black dust into the beam of the torch held shakily by David, forcing him to work one-handed.

"Now I've got to the second layer," panted Jenny. She inserted the chair leg and began to lever. "They seem to be looser. Hang on." Struggling amidst even more dust, she had caught sight of something bulky. "Shine the torch here, Dave. No – here!"

"I can't see—"

"There's something packed down."

"Hold the torch and maybe I can just reach." He pulled himself up, stretched out his arm – and gripped a damp bundle.

"The torch," he yelled. "Shine the torch."

"All right," Jenny protested. "I'm trying to." She was just as agitated.

There could be no doubt about it; they were both gazing at a bundle of old fifty pound notes.

"And there's more," breathed David.

In the end, he extracted another nine bundles, and they clambered down from the table, piling up the bank notes on its surface. They were damp and dirty and covered with cobwebs – but they were definitely real currency.

"Shall we count them?" asked David feverishly.

"Not here! We've got to get away before Len escapes."

Hunting around, David saw what he was looking for. "Here's a bag," he said.

"Wait a minute," said Jenny.

"What's up?"

"I recognise that. It's got a zip and it belonged to Arthur. Don't you remember, we saw him bringing it in – just before – just before he died."

David nodded. "Let's use it. Now where's Bert?"

They had been so concerned with searching for the money that they hadn't noticed the Labrador had disappeared.

They heard a muffled bark and Bert came bounding out of the tunnel, but he seemed very anxious and kept turning back to stare into the darkness.

"What is it?" whispered Jenny.

Feverishly scooping the bundles of notes into the decrepit old bag, David ignored them, hardly noticing the cold air that was beginning to filter into the shelter. Then the icy blast caught him unawares and he seemed to be falling into an Arctic abyss.

The shelter was brightly lit, paper chains adorned the ceiling and every surface was loaded with food.

Down each tunnel, trestle tables were laden with pies and cakes and bottles of beer and lemonade, and sitting at them were dozens of men and women and children wearing paper hats. Miss Perry and some of her pupils were on the top table and a photograph of Arthur was nailed to one of the wall props behind them, just under a couple of posters with Winston Churchill giving his V for Victory sign. The mayor was in the middle of a speech and his voice, distant at first, gradually became clearer.

But where was Jenny, wondered David anxiously. He couldn't see her anywhere. A wave of panic swept over him.

"And if it hadn't been for Arthur Jackson's generous gift we wouldn't be having this wonderful victory celebration today."

At his feet were piled the gas mask boxes, a number of ARP wardens' helmets, Home Guard uniforms and a road sign that read: TAKE COVER. AIR RAID IN PROGRESS. The mayor looked down and said, "All this stuff is very familiar to us now but it'll soon be part of a past that those of us here will always remember – a past in which Arthur Jackson died. And none of us will ever forget him either."

David saw Bert lying just under the mayor's feet, and, to his relief, Jenny was standing nearby.

"I remember Arthur saying to me," continued

the mayor, "before his untimely and premature death a few months ago, that if the Allies won the war, he'd left money in his will to throw a party for Hockley, down here in the shelter where we've all had to spend such difficult times. Well, this is it, my friends. Let's raise our glasses and give him a toast. To Arthur – our benefactor."

Everyone raised their glass. "To Arthur," and then someone shouted, "And to Bert."

The mayor said, "We've got a lot to thank him for in this neck of the woods, and naturally his faithful Labrador is being looked after at the Animal Sanctuary that Arthur always supported so generously. We're taking a collection for it today. And now, tuck in everybody."

A plate of succulent-looking jam tarts was beside David and he suddenly realised he was ravenously hungry. The tarts looked so tempting, with their crisp pastry fresh from the oven and deep-filled raspberry jam. He could even see the pips and began to imagine what it would be like to sink his teeth into the pulpy mass. David closed his eyes against the temptation but they appeared in his mind's eye, looking even more tempting, even more incredibly luscious than before. Arthur had really done them proud, he thought, and the people of Hockley had conjured up an incredible feast. If only he could just taste one tart – that would be enough. But, of course, he knew that it wouldn't. It never was.

It's the past, David told himself firmly. I mustn't interfere with the past or it will interfere with me. But that jam – that pastry – that taste— Temptation overcame him and he made a grab, but as he did so Jenny wrenched at his arm. "No," she yelled. "You know what'll happen."

But the bitterly cold taste was already in David's mouth and he cried out in pain, his teeth hurting and his throat so full of cold air that he couldn't breathe. He had never been so afraid and a great wall began to rush towards him – a wall that was black and shining with ice.

David opened his eyes and discovered that he and Jenny were back in the musty shelter and Bert was still staring down the tunnel as a powerful beam cut through the darkness.

"Hide," Jenny whispered.

But she was too late. Behind their torches, their gaunt faces looking deathly pale, were Gary, smiling triumphantly, and Len, grim-faced and angry-eyed.

CHAPTER THIRTEEN

"What you got in that bag?" Len snarled.

"You were after Arthur's money, weren't you?" David accused him.

"It weren't his. I was going to give it back to the bank. I've been searching for that cash for years. There's still a reward." He paused reflecting. "You two are going to be in dead trouble. Breaking into the school, obstructing an employee while on duty, entering an out of bounds area, trespassing, handling stolen property—"

"So you're nicked," interrupted Gary. "Properly nicked."

Bert growled, his hackles rose and he began to bark furiously. But he might as well not have been there – which to Len and Gary he wasn't.

"What's more, this shelter isn't safe," said Len suddenly. "I'm sure I saw one of the roof props shaking as we came down."

Jenny thought of their headlong flight through the tunnel last night. They had certainly cannoned into a good many of the props then and she could see that Len was as worried about the danger as he was furious about being locked into his office. But

Jenny was determined not to show her own anxiety.

"We're going to give the reward money to the Sanctuary," she said calmly.

"Come on," Len blustered. "Put that bag on the table."

David didn't move.

"Put it on the table," Len repeated.

"No way."

"I'm the school caretaker and you're trespassing on private property. I insist you pass that bag to me and I shall have it taken to the bank." Len sounded incredibly pompous and Jenny saw Gary grinning.

Len moved slowly and ponderously towards David who backed up hard against one of the props.

"Don't touch him," warned Jenny.

Len grabbed ineffectually at the bag, but David hung on to it and they struggled.

"Watch out," yelled Gary, the grin suddenly wiped off his face. "That prop's swaying."

"Get off it," shouted Jenny. "Both of you – move away." She was beside herself with fear and panic. "The ceiling's caving in."

Len stumbled away, David dived for cover but Jenny and Gary remained where they were, transfixed with fright as earth and rock began to fall with a terrible grinding, rending sound. Clouds of black dust followed and Gary and Len dropped their torches which were instantly buried in the falling debris.

Only David managed to hold on to his, the beam shining on the devastation as an eerie silence began to develop.

Suddenly, there came an ominous creaking sound.

"It's the roof," muttered Len. "The whole lot's going."

"What do we do now?" whined Gary.

Len ignored him. The dust clouds began to settle and they were able to see the extent of the damage, starkly revealed in the light of David's torch. "We'll never get out of here," he muttered desperately.

Gary began to cry while Jenny looked up at the roof, and the tons of earth and rock above them.

Arthur stepped from the last of the black clouds of dust, magnificent in a loud check overcoat. Bert padded over to him with a delighted bark.

David and Jenny didn't need the light of the torch to see them for Arthur and Bert now seemed to have a frosty outline, but the intense cold that normally preceded their ghostly appearances was absent. Instead the air in the shelter seemed to have become warmer.

The bag of money was half buried under a pile of earth, but Arthur went over to it unerringly, followed by Bert, wagging his tail.

"Dave?" The hoarse voice seemed to fill the shelter although he knew it was inside his head. "Jenny? Are you out there? Both of you?"

"We're here," said Jenny. "But there's been a roof fall and—"

"Take the bag," said Arthur's voice commandingly. "Put it in that kitchen stove. It'll be safe there – until you can come back. The reward has to go to the Sanctuary. Nowhere else."

David dragged the bag out of the debris and shone his torch into the eyes of Len Large and Gary. But they were standing still – so still that he knew they were frozen in time and that Arthur, in his desperation, had created some kind of limbo.

David opened the door of the battered and rusting stove and shoved the bag inside.

"I've got to go now," said Arthur and the twins could see that his frosty outline was dimmer.

"You can't leave us here." Jenny was incredulous. "You've got to help us. The roof is falling in. You can't just—"

"Bert," said the very faint voice. "You've got Bert."

Arthur's figure shimmered and went out like a spent candle.

★

The rumbling sound grew louder and David called Arthur's name over and over again.

Len was still beside himself with anxiety. "Who were you talking to then, eh?"

David didn't reply. Bert had disappeared and he was feeling very worried.

"We've got to get out," whined Gary.

"We've got to wait," said Jenny.

"What for?" demanded Len.

"Till the rumbling's stopped." David tried to divert him. "We've got to hang on until the tunnel stabilises."

"Suppose it doesn't," wailed Gary.

Len looked unsure and clearly he didn't know whether to agree with David or to take a decision himself. "Where's that bag with the money?" he asked in sudden concern.

"Must have got buried," said David a little too casually.

"No way." Gary was instantly suspicious. 'I'm sure I saw it sticking out of that pile of earth over there."

"Did you?"

"You know I did."

"Come on." Len was at his most officious now. "I hope you're not concealing stolen property. There will be very serious consequences for you if—"

But the props were trembling and creaking alarmingly.

"The whole lot's going," squealed Gary.

Len swore and David swung his torch up to the roof which was bulging horribly.

"We've got to get into one of the tunnels fast," he said.

But which one, wondered Jenny. Could Arthur help them? And where was Bert? For the first time she wanted to see them and realised to her horror that she had now resorted to relying on ghosts.

The ominous creaking sound was replaced by a rumbling and there was no sign of either Arthur or Bert. We've got to do something, thought David. We can't just stand here, being indecisive. A light patter of earth began to fall on his head and this was enough to send Gary hurtling for the nearest tunnel with a shrill scream, closely followed by a shambling Len Large.

"Come on," yelled Jenny. "We can't stick around."

"They may be going the wrong way," spluttered David.

"Too bad," she said and they both began to run. They were only just in time as the remainder of the shelter ceiling caved in, sending more earth, rock and choking black dust down into the kitchen and command post. Would the stove survive its burial, wondered Jenny. Or was the money lost for ever this time?

As the twins raced after the scurrying heels of Len and Gary, David realised with relief that he was the only torch bearer; at least he and Jenny had that advantage. He could hear them stumbling into something already, and a little later Gary gave a shrill cry of pain.

"Wait for us," David shouted.

"There's no way through." Len stood panting in the dusty, claustrophobic darkness.

Sure enough, when David's torch swept the tunnel, they could all see the heavy fall of rock.

"We'll have to go back," said Gary, shaking visibly. "Try the other tunnel."

But they were not given that chance. The roof behind them collapsed with a mighty roar.

"We're finished," observed Len in the ensuing silence and Gary began to sob. David and Jenny just felt numb as the torch's beam picked out the limits of their prison. They were in a small, high, cell-like area which was about three metres wide, and on either side the debris completely blocked their path. "We'll suffocate," continued Len hopelessly, and certainly the air did seem thin and stale.

David heard singing and, glancing at Jenny, knew that she had suddenly become aware of it too. The sound was coming from a little way ahead of them, behind the rock fall that blocked their way to the exit. It was thin and faint but just audible.

We'll meet again, don't know where, don't know when,
But I know we'll meet again some sunny day;
Keep smiling through, just like you always do,
Till the blue skies drive the dark clouds far away.

"I'm seeing double," muttered Jenny.

"What?" sobbed Gary.

"Nothing," said David. But he was seeing double too.

The twins could hear a buzz bomb falling as they watched the wartime ghosts sitting on their benches in the tunnel, singing through the silences and as explosion after explosion rocked the shelter.

They were all there – Miss Perry and her pupils, the locals, the warden, even Ron and Arthur. It was a time when they were all alive – a glorious time, thought Jenny. Some of the women were sewing hooks on blackout curtains, and Arthur and Ron, clearly in uneasy alliance, were drinking cups of tea and talking to each other. Ironically, just over their heads, the familiar notice read: CARE-LESS TALK COSTS LIVES. Bert was at Arthur's feet, his head on his paws, his eyes closed.

"They can't help us," whispered David.

"They've got to," said Jenny.

Bert got lazily to his feet and the vision disappeared.

★

The earth began to fall on them again. Gary was sobbing uncontrollably now.

"This is it then," Len muttered.

"That earth isn't coming from the roof," Jenny said. "It's falling from that hole – there's a gap, right up there between the rubble and the roof."

"I don't get it." Len was utterly bewildered.

"I think it's Bert," blurted out David. "I—"

"Who?" shrieked Gary.

"Nothing. Nobody," David said quickly as he ran the torch over the barrier, searching out the gap again.

"We've got to get through," said Jenny. "Now. Before it fills in or the roof here comes down."

"Go up there?" Len was horrified. "It's un-stable."

"So is everywhere else," yelled David.

"Well—"

"Come on." Gary began to climb up the mound. "I don't want to die down here."

But Arthur did, thought Jenny, remembering him for the first time with affection rather than dread.

Slowly, laboriously, fearfully, they all followed Gary.

"Can you squeeze through?" David played his torch around Gary's ankles which were waving in the air.

130

"Just. But I don't know what's on t..
side," he wailed. "Can't you pass the
through?"

"No. The others need to see by it."

"I could be going anywhere," came Gary's
muffled voice.

Len Large made even more of a fuss as David,
precariously balanced on the fallen debris, shakily
shone the torch on the gap.

"I won't fit," Len panted. "I'll never be able to
squeeze through."

"You'll have to try."

"I can't."

"You've got to, Mr Large," insisted David. "If
you don't—" But he didn't have to finish the
sentence; somehow Len squeezed himself into the
gap and, gasping for breath, managed to pull
himself along behind Gary.

"You OK, Dave?" asked Jenny as she scrambled
up to join him.

"Yes. I just hope the rest of the roof hasn't fallen
in."

"Bert wouldn't trick us."

"He might not know," replied David in a
hollow voice.

"Ghosts do know. And haven't you noticed –
it's not cold any more and Bert and Arthur are still
around."

"Maybe they've accepted us," he said quietly.

metres to go, David's haphazardly spiralling torch momentarily lit up the bulging roof.

"Run!" she yelled. "Run faster."

The light ahead widened, she could smell fresh air, the dust was less choking, her watering eyes could see sunlight. Then Jenny was on the threshold, stumbling up the steps into the playground, hardly believing that they had escaped. They? She could see Gary. But where was David? He had been right behind her seconds earlier but he wasn't now. And neither was Len Large.

Jenny turned round and ran straight back into the shelter and down the collapsing tunnel she had just come up, cursing herself for not watching her twin all the time, for not making sure he was beside her. The debris was falling even faster now and a large stone hit her a glancing blow, making her howl with pain. Then she tripped over something soft and screamed, the panic surging through her, raw and uncontrolled.

"It's me," snapped David.

"What are you doing?"

"Len's passed out. I think a rock hit him. There's blood and – I've tried to drag him but he's so heavy."

"Let me help." Somehow Jenny found and grabbed one of Len's arms. Choking and gasping the twins managed to pull him from the roaring, painful, falling darkness into daylight and safety.

Blackened and filthy, David lay on the ground, gasping and wheezing, wondering where Jenny had gone. Beside him Gary was in a similar condition while Len, conscious again, tried to lever himself to his feet. He was muttering something.

"I've got to find it." He dragged himself up as people began to flood into the playground, alarmed by the roar of the falling shelter.

Where was Jenny, wondered David over and over again as he struggled to his feet. Surely she couldn't have run back into the shelter again? He stared at it in horror, for where the entrance had been there was now only a black and billowing cloud.

"Jenny!" David yelled as a neighbour he vaguely recognised tried to make him sit down again. "Jenny!" Then he was almost hurled flat by a freezing blast of deadening cold air as Bert emerged from the wreckage. But he was not heading for David; instead, he loped towards Len Large who was still staggering towards the shelter with an intent expression on his face. The blast struck him and he spun round, a look of utter bewilderment and horror on his face. "Hell Hound," he muttered and fell over in a heap just as a police siren began to wail.

"Jenny," yelled David desperately. "Jenny.

Where are you?" The intense cold was withdrawing but Bert was ahead of him, running towards the piles of broken masonry and rock and earth that was all that remained of the shelter. Then David saw his twin gazing down at a hole in the rubble. Battered, covered in debris but still intact was the stove where they had hidden Arthur's money.

"You can't go over there, young man," yelled someone, but David and Bert were running towards the hole into which Jenny was already clambering. She dragged open the door of the stove – and pulled out Arthur's bulging old bag.

EPILOGUE

David and Jenny stood under the old oak tree the following Sunday evening. They were very tired and had had to answer many questions from the police and Mr Decker and their parents and sometimes all three at the same time. But the story they had agreed on – that they had heard a rumour Arthur had stowed the money in the air raid shelter and that they had managed to recover it – was eventually accepted, despite the fact they were all too vague about the source of the rumour. But the twins had been delighted to hear that the bank had agreed to give a substantial reward to the Sanctuary which saved it from bankruptcy. The bad news was that David and Jenny were in serious trouble for trespassing and exposing themselves to danger.

Annoyingly, Len Large and Gary, who had both claimed to have seen the twins entering the shelter and instantly rushed to rescue them, were believed and seen as heroes. Len had claimed he had seen Gary running to the rescue first and had followed him in after issuing a warning that was ignored.

Mrs Golding unwittingly supplied the reason for

Len's interest in the air raid shelter, when she mentioned in passing that his eldest brother Ron had once been a friend of Arthur's. That explained a lot, the twins thought. But at least they'd been able to prevent Len and Gary from getting their greedy hands on the money.

An evening wind was gently rustling the leaves on the ancient bough of the oak tree.

"Maybe it's whispering to us," said David.

Then the twins realised that the tree was doing just that and eventually recognised the words:

"We'll meet again, don't know where, don't know when—"

This time there was no cold air; in fact the evening seemed to grow a little warmer as Arthur and Bert strolled in to the playground. Arthur knelt down and took Bert's head in his hands, rumpling his fur and kissing his nose. Then their images abruptly faded away into a pool of mellow light as the sun went down.